the Return of
Santa Paws

Don't miss the first book starring the lovable dog hero, *SANTA PAWS*

the Return of Santa Paws

by
Nicholas Edwards

AN
APPLE
PAPERBACK

SCHOLASTIC INC.
New York Toronto London Auckland Sydney

ISBN 0-590-94471-1

24 23 22 21 20 19 18 17 16 15   23/0

Printed in the U.S.A.   40

First Scholastic printing, November 1996

the Return of
Santa Paws

1

The dog was happy every day. Eating food was his very favorite thing to do, but sleeping was a lot of fun, too. More than anything else, of course, he loved his owners, the Callahans. After living on the streets for a long, lonely time, he had finally found a family who wanted to adopt him. Now he had a warm bed to sleep on every night, fresh water in a red plastic dish that was just for him, and Milk-Bones *all day long*!

The Callahans were the nicest people in the world. Mr. Callahan was a writer, and so the dog spent most of the day following him around the house. Mrs. Callahan taught physics at Ocean-port High School, and the dog liked her because she was almost always the one who fed him and brushed him. Sometimes she would also take him to the vet, but he didn't really mind. The vet was a nice person, too.

But the dog *especially* loved Gregory and

Patricia, the Callahans' children. Gregory was eleven years old and in the sixth grade, while Patricia had just started junior high this year. They took him for lots of walks, taught him tricks, and fed him snacks under the dinner table. The dog *really* liked snacks.

While Gregory and Patricia were at school, the dog usually slept under Mr. Callahan's desk. Sometimes Mr. Callahan would sit down at the desk, mutter to himself, and then pound wildly on his keyboard for awhile. On other days, he would lie on the couch and watch television, or spend hours blaring music and pacing back and forth. No matter what Mr. Callahan was doing, though, he liked to talk to himself. The dog wasn't always sure what he was saying, but he would listen, anyway, and wag his tail a lot.

When Mr. Callahan was working hard and the dog got bored, he would play with Evelyn, the family's tiger cat. If she didn't feel like playing, he would chase her until she whacked him on the nose with her paw. When that happened, the dog would always yelp and whimper a little. Mr. Callahan would come out to see what was wrong and then give them each a treat. After eating his treat, the dog would be happy again. Then he and Evelyn would lie down and sleep some more.

Everyone in the family called him by a different name. His real name was Nicholas, but they almost never used that. The dog thought it was fun to have lots of nicknames, and he answered to all of them. Mr. Callahan always called him "Pumpkin," and Evelyn was "the little Pumpkin."

Mrs. Callahan referred to him as "Smart-Guy." When he tipped over the trash, she would look stern and ask, "Are you the one who did this, Smart-Guy?" If Patricia was around, she would say, "No way, Mom — it was Greg." The dog would just stand there, and wag his tail, and lift his right paw in the most charming way he could. The family always liked it when he did tricks.

Patricia had taught him to answer to "Princess" and "Sweetpea," because it made Gregory mad. Gregory usually called him "Nick" or "Nicky" or "Bud." Evelyn, the cat, didn't really talk to him much, but the dog was pretty sure she thought of him as "Hey, you!"

But the truth was, that the Callahans — along with everyone else in town — called him "Santa Paws" more than anything else. He had shown up in town the Christmas before, and somehow, the name stuck. The dog wasn't sure why he liked that name so much, but he would wag his tail extra hard whenever anyone said "Santa Paws." There was something really *friendly* about that name.

The only thing he didn't like people to say to him was "bad dog." It didn't happen very often, but whenever he heard "bad dog," he would slump down with his tail between his legs. Usually, the person who said it, would come and pat him right away and he would feel better. He tried to be good all of the time, and not chew shoes or break anything. That way, they would just say, "What a good dog!" Whenever he heard those magic words, he would jump around and bark a lot.

Sometimes, when he and the Callahans were riding in the car, people in other cars would wave and shout, "Hi, Santa Paws!" out the window. If they were taking him for a walk, people they passed would always yell, "Look, there's Santa Paws!" Then they would smile, and sometimes even clap.

Gregory thought it was really cool that everyone in Oceanport loved their dog so much, but Patricia was always embarrassed. As far as she was concerned, all of that attention wasn't dignified. Patricia *liked* to be dignified, no matter what. Gregory didn't care, one way or the other.

Every day, the dog slept until he heard Gregory and Patricia coming up the back steps. Then he would scramble to his feet and dash out of Mr. Callahan's office. By the time they opened the door, he would be standing in the kitchen to greet them. Right after they got home, they always liked to sit down at the table and have a snack. One of them would also give him a Milk-Bone, so he could keep them company.

It was almost Christmas, and Gregory and Patricia couldn't wait for their vacation to start. There were only two days of school left before they had a whole week off. The family was going to spend the holidays up at their grandparents' lake cabin in Vermont, and they were all really looking forward to the trip.

It had snowed twice in the last week, and the backyard was still covered with about five inches of soft slush. Gregory and Patricia were just coming home from school, and they had been bickering for several blocks. Their fights were never very serious, but they liked to have *lots* of them, just to keep in practice. At least, that's what Patricia always told their parents.

"It's *really* cold," Gregory said, for at least the tenth time. He was all bundled-up in three layers of clothes — a down jacket, a Red Sox cap, and thick ragg-wool mittens, but he was still freezing.

"It is not," Patricia said — *also* for the tenth time. Her New England Patriots jacket wasn't even zipped, and her black beret was *purely* a fashion statement. She was wearing an oversized pair of red mirrored sunglasses, too. "You're just a big baby."

"*You're* a big faker," Gregory responded. "If you were, like, by yourself, I bet you'd be all shivering, and running really fast so you'd get home quicker."

Patricia shook her head. "No way. I'm too cool to be cold."

Gregory thought about that. As far as he was concerned, *nobody* was that cool — not even Patricia. "You know what would be cool?" he asked reflectively. "If I put a whole bunch of snow down your back."

Patricia stopped walking long enough to scowl at him. "If you do, I'll put a whole bunch in your *bed*. Under the blankets, inside your pillow, and everything."

Gregory grinned at her. "Oh, yeah? Then I'll put snow in all your shoes. Especially your cowboy boots."

"Then *I'll* cover your computer with snow," Patricia said, grinning now, too. "Inside your disc drive, smash it onto your keyboard, send it through the printer — you name it."

This was the kind of fight that really upset their parents, who never seemed to understand that they were mostly just kidding. *Mostly*, anyway.

The two of them looked so much alike, with

dark brown hair and very blue eyes, that people were always asking if they were twins. He *wishes* he could be so lucky, Patricia would say. She's *way* uglier, Gregory would say.

They turned the corner, and the icy wind coming up from the ocean whipped toward them. Their house was at the end of the block, and they both walked more quickly.

"I bet the windchill's about thirty-five below," Gregory guessed.

"Give me a break, Greg. It's probably twenty *above*," Patricia said.

Gregory looked over at her dubiously. "Are you really not cold?"

"Well, maybe a little," Patricia admitted, and she zipped her jacket halfway.

Gregory laughed. "I knew you were faking."

Patricia shrugged self-consciously. "So I'm faking, so what?"

Gregory just laughed.

The weekend before, the whole family had put up their Christmas decorations, and the house looked really pretty. There were wreaths on the front and back doors, and Mr. Callahan had hung lights on the pine tree in the side yard. Their Christmas tree was in the living room, right in front of the bay windows. That way, at night, everyone who drove by the house could look inside and see it.

"Did you spend all your Christmas money?" Gregory asked.

Patricia nodded. "Most of it. Why?"

"I spent all mine, and I didn't get a present for the baby yet," Gregory said.

The baby was Miranda, their cousin. She was almost exactly a year old now, and had just started talking. Miranda's parents were their Uncle Steve, and Aunt Emily. Uncle Steve was their father's little brother, and he was a police officer in the Oceanport department. Their Aunt Emily was an advertising executive at a big firm in Boston. After the baby was born, she had arranged it so that she could work at home two days a week, and commute into the city on the other three days.

"I've only got about eight-fifty left," Patricia said, "but you can borrow it, if you want."

Patricia might tease him a lot, but she was actually really, really nice, when no one was looking. "Thanks. What did you get her?" Gregory asked.

Patricia shrugged. "Sunglasses. What else?"

As they started down the shoveled walk to the back door, they could hear delighted barking from inside the house.

"It's the Princess!" Patricia said cheerfully. "She's waiting for us!"

Gregory was not amused. "Don't call him that — it's dumb."

Patricia laughed. "Oh, what, and *Santa Paws* isn't? Come on, Greg. Get serious."

"Call him Nick," Gregory said. "He likes Nick."

"He likes *everything*, Greg," Patricia pointed out.

That was actually true, so Gregory just opened the back door instead of arguing. Whenever he was at school, he spent a lot of time thinking about his dog and wondering how he was. It was always a relief to get home and be able to play with him. Lots of people had nice dogs — but their dog was *special*.

Gregory poked his head around the edge of the door without going inside. "Where's my pal?" he asked.

The dog barked and pawed eagerly at the door.

"He waits here the whole time for me to come home, just like Lassie," Gregory told Patricia.

Patricia shook her head. "No way, he just gets up when he hears us coming. I think he takes naps all day."

"No, he waits," Gregory insisted. "Kind of like a sentry."

"Yeah," Patricia said. "Sure."

As they came inside, the dog kept barking. He wagged his tail back and forth, and jumped up on his hind legs to greet them. He had finally stopped growing, but at eighty-five pounds, he was a *big* dog. Patricia was small for her age

9

and weighed about the same, so sometimes he knocked her down by accident.

Gregory, on the other hand, was pretty tall, and outweighed both of them. He only had an advantage of about seven pounds, but he figured that it still counted. His parents had given him some light barbells for his birthday, and he did thirty repetitions every morning when he got up, and then again before he went to bed. He and his best friend Oscar did lots of endurance exercises, too, so that when they got to high school, they would be able to make the football team.

Naturally, Patricia's reaction to this was, "Yeah. You *wish*." Sometimes, she and *her* best friend Rachel did a few abdominal crunches, but that was about it. The rest of the time, they just ate Doritos and drank Cokes.

The dog had lifted his front paws up onto Gregory's shoulders, so Gregory danced him around the kitchen a little.

"What a good dog," he said proudly. "You're the *best* dog, Nicky."

The dog barked and wagged his tail.

"Are you going to have a Milk-Bone?" Gregory asked.

The dog barked more loudly.

"Okay." Gregory stopped dancing with him, and then took off his jacket. "Let's get you a Milk-Bone."

The dog wagged his tail so hard that his whole body shook. He loved Gregory! He loved Patricia! He loved his life! He loved *Milk-Bones*!

What a great day!

2

Gregory and Patricia hung up their coats on the hooks behind the door, and dropped their knapsacks on the kitchen table. In the meantime, the dog ran around in circles, barking every so often. Since he was a German shepherd and collie mix, he had a very deep and commanding bark.

"Are you hungry, Greg?" Patricia asked.

"I'm *starved*," Gregory said.

Patricia nodded. "Me, too," she said, and opened the refrigerator.

Gregory picked up the plastic dish on the floor and carried it over to the sink. He dumped out the old water and filled it with fresh water.

The dog wagged his tail cooperatively and drank some right away. It tasted *really* good. Nice and cold.

While Gregory took out the box of Milk-Bones, Patricia studied the food inside the refrigerator.

"There's a whole lot of carrot sticks, and yogurt, and stuff," she said without much enthusiasm.

"Well, you know, you're a girl, so you like, need lots of calcium," Gregory said. He'd read in magazines that women were supposed to get more calcium than men. "So your bones don't get weird."

Patricia shook her head. "No, what I need right now, is *candy*. Or — fudge, maybe. Fudge would be good."

She opened a plastic container and looked inside. Beef stew. She closed the container, and checked another. This one had leftover macaroni and cheese, and she set it out on the counter, along with some butterscotch pudding their mother had fixed the night before.

"We could make popcorn?" Gregory suggested.

"Yeah, that'd be all right," Patricia agreed. "And maybe some hot chocolate."

They could hear music playing loudly in the den, and they both stopped to listen for a minute.

"Frank," Patricia said grimly.

Gregory nodded. As usual, their father was listening to Frank Sinatra. Sometimes, he would put on Billie Holiday or Ella Fitzgerald, but mostly it was Frank, Frank, *Frank*. Endless hours of *Frank*. "Is he singing?" he asked.

They listened again. If their father was singing along, that generally meant that he wasn't getting any work done.

"No," Patricia decided. "Just listening."

"Good," Gregory said, relieved. When their father's writing was going well, they could do whatever they wanted and never get in trouble. When he had writer's block, he was much more strict.

Patricia started fixing dishes of macaroni and cheese to put in the microwave, and then stopped. "Hey, I know!" she said. "Let's go see what he's wearing!"

Gregory's eyes lit up. "Yeah!" he agreed.

When they left for school in the morning, their father would usually be wearing pajama bottoms and an old college T-shirt. Then sometimes, during the day, he would change into outfits that he thought might help him get in the mood to write better.

"Be really quiet," Patricia said softly, as they crept through the living room. "So he doesn't hear us coming."

The music was so loud there was no *way* he would hear them, but Gregory nodded anyway. If their father knew they were sneaking up on him, he would have time to whip off any goofy hats or other silly things he might be wearing.

The dog barked and galloped ahead of them. He ran so fast that he slipped on a small braided rug and skidded into a nearby wall.

"Santa Paws, shhh!" Patricia said, and then

frowned. "Did I just forget and call him Santa Paws?"

Gregory nodded.

"Hit me next time," Patricia said.

He wasn't about to pass *that* up. "Absolutely!" Gregory promised.

When they got to the den door, they could see their father sitting at his word processor with his back to them. Computers were too mod for him. His posture was very straight and he was holding his hands motionless above the keyboard, as though he *might* start writing at any second.

Gregory and Patricia tried not to laugh when they saw that he had on a top hat and a black bow tie. Once they had caught him wearing a bright green sombrero, because he was writing a scene set in Mexico. Right now, he also had on gray sweatpants and a T-shirt with a picture of the Grinch on it.

"Bunny slippers?" Patricia whispered.

Gregory peered underneath the desk. "No, *Snoopy* slippers," he whispered back, and they both snickered. Lots of times, Mr. Callahan forgot and went out in public with his slippers on. People in Oceanport seemed to think that this was — quaint.

They waited to see if he was going to type anything, and when he didn't, they started singing, "You Make Me Feel So Young" along with Frank. Over the years, completely by accident, they had learned all of the words to an astonishing number of old songs. Their mother mostly played musicals, so they were pretty strong on those, too. When Patricia's science teacher had asked her recently to explain the concept of "osmosis," she had used their uncanny knowledge of song lyrics as an example. Her teacher had found this to be a very clever comparison, and gave her an *A* for the day.

The dog started barking again, because he *liked* singing. Singing was funny.

Mr. Callahan turned around to look at them. "You two are home early," he said, sounding surprised.

Actually, they were *late*, because Patricia had forgotten her global studies book and they had to go back to get it.

"You want to hear 'Moonlight in Vermont?' " Gregory asked. "We're good at that one, too."

Mr. Callahan smiled, saved whatever he was writing on a disk, and then stood up. Their cat, Evelyn, who had been sleeping soundly on his lap, was quite annoyed by this. She flounced over to the couch, and curled up again.

"How was school?" Mr. Callahan asked. "Are you kids hungry?"

"Fine," Patricia said, just as Gregory said, "*Yes.*"

Realizing that he was still wearing his top hat,

Mr. Callahan frowned and took it off. "Ballroom scene," he explained.

Patricia and Gregory shrugged politely, doing their best not to laugh again. However, they failed miserably.

"Dad, does Nicholas wait all day for me by the door?" Gregory asked as they walked to the kitchen. "Because he misses me so much?"

"Hmmm?" Mr. Callahan said vaguely. "Oh." He paused, and then didn't quite make eye contact. "Well, sure. I mean, yes. No question about it. Sits there nonstop. Never moves."

"That means no," Patricia said to Gregory.

Mr. Callahan examined the plastic containers on the kitchen counter. He was over six feet tall, with greying hair that was almost always rumpled. He wore thick brown glasses, and usually slouched when he walked.

"This looks good," he said, taking down a plate for himself and spooning out some cold macaroni and cheese. "But try not to spoil your appetites, okay? We're meeting your aunt and uncle for dinner at six-thirty."

"Italian?" Gregory asked. Italian food was his favorite.

"How about Mexican?" Patricia suggested. "We haven't had Mexican for a while."

"Rumor has it, it's going to be Chinese," their father answered.

It was a safe bet that that rumor had come straight from their *mother*.

They had finished the macaroni and cheese, and were halfway through the beef stew, when Mrs. Callahan got home. She was carrying an oversized canvas briefcase and several bulging shopping bags.

"Hi, Mom. Are those Christmas presents?" Gregory asked.

Quickly, Mrs. Callahan held the bags behind her back. "No," she said, and grinned at them. "Whatever gave you that idea?"

The dog had been sitting alertly next to Gregory, in case a piece of beef from the stew fell on the floor by accident. Smelling something familiar, he got up and went over to sniff the bags. A rawhide chew bone! He was almost *sure* that he smelled a rawhide chew bone.

"No, it's a surprise, Santa Paws," Mrs. Callahan said, and lifted the bag up out of his reach. "Go lie down."

Lie down. He knew what "lie down" meant, but right now, he wanted to sit. If he went over to lie down on his special rug, he might forget about the beef stew and fall asleep. So he sat down next to Gregory's chair and lifted his paw, instead.

"That's good," Mrs. Callahan told him. "You're a very good dog."

She thought he was good. Yay! The dog

18

wagged his tail, and then returned his attention to the beef stew. So far, he had managed to catch a piece of potato Mr. Callahan dropped, and he had snapped up two chunks of meat Gregory had slipped under the table.

Mrs. Callahan glanced up at the kitchen clock, and then at her husband. "We're supposed to meet Steve and Emily and the baby in about an hour and a half," she reminded him. "Maybe you all should save some room for supper."

"It's just a snack, Mom," Patricia said.

Mr. Callahan looked a little sheepish. "A *hearty* snack," he admitted.

"Whatever you say." Mrs. Callahan started out of the room with her bags, then paused. "Did anyone feed the dog?"

The dog leaped enthusiastically to his feet again. "Feed the dog" was another one of the magic phrases, right up there with "ride in the car."

"We were about to," Gregory said.

Evelyn came ambling out from the direction of the living room. She jumped up on the side counter where her small green dish was kept and meowed loudly — and sadly.

"I'll bet you were about to feed her, too," Mrs. Callahan said. "And maybe even clean up these dishes, while you're at it."

Gregory nodded. "Yep."

"Right away," Patricia promised.

Mr. Callahan was already on his feet and heading for the sink. "Count on it."

"I thought so," Mrs. Callahan said, and then she disappeared up the stairs with her many mysterious shopping bags.

When it was time to leave for dinner, the dog watched with worried eyes as the Callahans put on their hats, coats, and gloves. Where were they going? Was he going to be left alone? Would they be back soon? This was *horrible*. He slumped down on the floor and rested his muzzle miserably on his front paws.

"Can Nicholas come?" Gregory asked. He really hated to go *anywhere* without his dog.

Hearing his name — *one* of his names, anyway — the dog's ears pricked forward.

"I don't know, Greg," his mother answered. "It's pretty cold out there, and it might not be a good idea for him to wait in the car."

"But he always comes," Patricia reminded her.

Mrs. Callahan nodded. "Okay. Bring one of the beach towels, though, so he has someplace to curl up."

When the dog saw Gregory open the cupboard and take out a thick blue towel, he stood up tentatively. Was the towel for him? Was he going to have a bath, maybe?

"Want to come for a ride in the car?" Gregory asked.

A ride in the car! His favorite! The dog barked, and then chased his tail for a minute to show how happy he was.

Next to eating — and sleeping — riding in the car was the best thing in the whole world!

3

The best part of being in the car was when one of the Callahans would roll down the window, and he could smell lots of exciting scents. But he also liked just sitting and watching objects flash by. Usually they drove to interesting places, like the beach or the city, and there was always something new to see.

When they were at stores and the dog was waiting for them to come back, he liked to sneak up into the front seat. It was fun to sit in the driver's seat and gaze out through the windshield. Then, when he saw them coming back, he would quickly jump into the back again. Most of the time, he got caught, but no one ever really got mad at him, so he figured it was okay.

Oceanport always looked very pretty during Christmas. It was a small town, and the streets twinkled with bright strings of lights. All of the stores and restaurants and office buildings would put up festive decorations, and every year, there was a contest to decide who had done the most beautiful job.

During the holiday season, the municipal park had lots of special exhibits, which were called "The Festival of Many Lands." The exhibits were devoted to all kinds of different cultures, religions, and other traditions. Oceanport was proud of being a very democratic and multicultural town.

When the dog had been a lonely stray the year before, he had slept in Santa's sleigh in the park. Some of the local townspeople had noticed him there, and they had given him the name "Santa Paws." That was before he had an owner, and he was always cold and sad and hungry. He ran into a lot of people who were in trouble, and he did his best to help them, so the name "Santa Paws" seemed perfect for him. The dog was just glad when he met Gregory and Patricia, and got to go live with them. He was *still* always hungry, though!

The Chinese restaurant was right on Main Street, and Mr. Callahan found a parking place a few doors away.

"Can we walk down to the park for a minute?" Gregory asked, as they got out of the car.

"*May* you," Mrs. Callahan corrected him automatically. "Why don't we go after supper and look at the decorations?"

Gregory nodded, and carefully unrolled one of

the back windows a couple of inches so that Santa Paws would have plenty of fresh air. Then he patted him, and started to close the door.

Suddenly sensing that something was wrong, the dog stood up on the seat to look outside. The fur rose on his back and he sniffed the air uneasily, trying to figure out what was happening. He knew that there was trouble brewing somewhere — he just wasn't sure what it was.

"What is it, boy?" Gregory asked.

Across the street, Mrs. Lowell had just come out of Mabel's Five-and-Dime, carrying lots of bundles. Her four-year-old daughter Bethany was skipping along next to her, bouncing a miniature Shaquille O'Neal basketball.

The sidewalk was a little bit icy, and Mrs. Lowell slipped. She dropped most of her packages and had to bend over to pick them up. As she did, Bethany's ball bounced off a chunk of snow and rolled right into the busy street!

Bethany gasped and ran after her beloved basketball, without looking both ways first.

Seeing this, the dog leaped out of the car. Barking loudly, he raced across the street, dodging traffic. Horns beeped, and cars skidded on the ice, as people tried to steer out of the way.

"Hey!" Gregory yelled. "Look out!" He started

to chase after his dog, but there were too many cars.

The man driving the car closest to Bethany jammed on his brakes, but the car spun out of control, and headed directly toward her! Everyone on the sidewalks was frozen with shock.

The dog grabbed Bethany's hood with his teeth, and dragged her out of the way at the last second. He pulled her safely between two parked cars and then gently released her hood and nudged her to her feet.

With that accomplished, he bolted back into the street to fetch the basketball. The ball was too big to fit in his mouth, so he used his nose to roll it in front of him. He deposited the ball at Bethany's feet, and then stood there, wagging his tail.

All around them, people were running across the street and jumping out of their cars to see what had happened. Everyone was very upset, and expecting the worst.

Mrs. Lowell and Gregory reached the pair first.

"Oh, thank God," Mrs. Lowell breathed, and she hugged her little daughter tightly.

Bethany smiled up at her, not even bruised by her narrow escape. "Santa Paws saved me!" she said happily. "He's Santa's best helper!"

Mrs. Lowell hugged her closer, so relieved that she couldn't even speak.

"You all right, boy?" Gregory asked the dog. Then he swiftly checked him over, running his hands over the dog's back and legs to make sure he hadn't been injured.

The dog barked once, and wagged his tail. He really liked being patted.

Patricia and their parents rushed over to join them.

"Are they okay?" Patricia asked.

Gregory nodded. "Everybody's fine."

Hearing that, most of the people who had gathered nearby began to applaud.

"Hooray for Santa Paws!" Mabel from the Five-and-Dime store hollered, and a few people cheered.

"I don't know how to thank all of you," Mrs. Lowell said to the Callahans. "If it weren't for your wonderful dog — " She stopped, overcome again.

Gregory always carried extra biscuits in his pockets, and he took one out.

The dog barked and joyfully accepted it. He crunched up the biscuit right away, his tail thumping against one of the parked cars. No matter how many Milk-Bones he ate, he was still always surprised by how delicious they were!

"You know," Mr. Callahan said thoughtfully to his wife, "he really *is* a good dog."

It was hard to disagree with that, so Mrs. Callahan just nodded.

Mr. Callahan's brother Steve had come out of the Chinese restaurant to see what all of the excitement was about. As far as he was concerned, a police officer was *never* really off-duty, and so he liked to keep an eye on things.

"What's going on?" he asked, sounding both curious and authoritative. "Everyone all right?" Uncle Steve wasn't quite as tall as Mr. Callahan, but he was a lot more muscular. He was only thirty-two and unlike Mr. Callahan, his hair hadn't started turning grey yet. Even so, it was easy to see that they were related.

"Thanks to Santa Paws!" someone shouted.

"Oh." Uncle Steve looked around and saw that everything seemed to be fine. "Okay. Good."

Patricia moved to stand next to him, folding her arms decisively across her chest. She was pretty sure that she wanted to be a police officer, too, when she grew up — that is, unless she could be a member of the Supreme Court. "Should we tell them to move along, and go about their business, Uncle Steve?" she asked.

Uncle Steve laughed, and reached out to give her ponytail a little flip. "No, it's okay, Patty. I think they'll figure out that one for themselves."

The family who owned the Chinese restaurant had come outside, too. Their last name was Lee, and their son Tom was also a member of the Oceanport Police Department. Because of that, most of the police officers in town ate at their restaurant regularly. Of course, it didn't hurt that the food was *really* good.

"Was it Santa Paws again?" Mr. Lee asked the crowd in general.

Most of the bystanders nodded, and some of them started clapping again.

Mrs. Lee smiled at the Callahans. "We would be delighted to have the hero dine in our restaurant tonight."

Gregory looked surprised. "Wait, you mean, inside? *With* us?"

Mrs. Lee nodded, and held the door open with a flourish. "Please. We would be very honored."

"Whoa," Patricia said, impressed. "That is like, *so* European."

"We will prepare our finest meat dish for him," Mr. Lee proclaimed grandly. "Please, follow me."

As they walked inside, Mr. Callahan leaned over to his wife again. "If it's their very finest dish, think a certain dog will be willing to *share* it with us?" he asked in a low voice.

Mrs. Callahan laughed. "Well, maybe if you ask nicely. . . ."

The dog couldn't believe that he was being allowed to go inside the restaurant, instead of waiting in the car like always. How fun! He trotted happily next to Gregory, waving his tail back and forth.

Mr. Lee led them over to the best table in the restaurant. Gregory and Patricia's aunt Emily was already sitting there with her baby, Miranda. Miranda was wearing a red velvet holiday dress, with black patent leather shoes, and she looked even more adorable than usual.

The Lees' teenage daughter, Nancy, brought out a special rug from the back room, which Santa Paws immediately sat on. He knew that small rugs were almost always meant just for him. This one was very soft and comfortable, with nice fancy patterns, and he woofed once before settling down.

Mr. Lee distributed menus, while Mrs. Lee filled their water glasses.

"Tonight, everything is on the house!" Mr. Lee announced. "Out of respect for the heroic Santa Paws!"

"Oh, no," Mrs. Callahan protested. "We couldn't — "

"We *insist*," Mrs. Lee said. "Consider it our holiday gesture."

Gregory nudged Patricia's arm. "So, should we order lobster, and shrimp, and all?" he whispered, since those were the most expensive items on the menu.

"Don't be a jerk," she whispered back. "Besides, Mom and Dad'll leave a *really* big tip, so it'll work out pretty much the same."

Gregory nodded and looked down at his menu. His favorites were Hunan flower steak and General Tso's chicken, anyway. Patricia almost always ordered broccoli with garlic sauce, because, she would explain, of the considerable health benefits. Mr. and Mrs. Callahan always laughed when she said things like that. Gregory and Patricia were never exactly sure what was so funny, and they would write it off to parental foolishness.

"So," Aunt Emily said, once they had all been served tea, and soda, and other drinks. "What should we toast to?"

"Santa Paws," Gregory said. "Who else?"

They all raised their cups and glasses. Miranda giggled and imitated them by holding up her bottle.

"Okay, Mr. Writer," Uncle Steve said to Mr. Callahan. "Let's see how profound you are."

Mr. Callahan frowned. Sometimes, under pressure, he lapsed into writer's block. "To Santa Paws," he said finally. "The best dog in Oceanport!"

"The best dog on the Eastern seaboard," Patricia corrected him.

"The best dog in the *world*," Gregory said.

They all drank to that, and then started in on their scallion pancakes and other appetizers.

The dog wagged his tail when Patricia gave him some pork strips on a small white plate. He had no idea why they were celebrating tonight, but he was certainly having a very nice time!

4

Over dinner, they all talked about their Christmas plans. Patricia and Gregory's grandparents lived in Montpelier, Vermont, but they also had a lake cabin in the Northeast Kingdom of Vermont, up near the Canadian border. It was winterized, and so this year, they were going to spend the holidays there. The drive from Boston was pretty long, but the cabin was right on a beautiful lake. There was skiing nearby, and plenty of other winter sports available.

"When are you all heading up?" Mrs. Callahan asked Uncle Steve and Aunt Emily.

Steve shook his head. "Emily's going to drive up with the baby, and take the week up there, but I have to work on Christmas, so I'm going to fly."

Hearing that, Gregory and Patricia perked up. They loved flying in their uncle's plane. He was a private pilot, and he shared a little Cessna Skyhawk with an old friend of his from the Army. Uncle Steve really loved baseball, and during the summer, he would fly all over New England and upstate New York to go to minor league games in tiny little towns. Lots of times, Gregory and Patricia would get to go along. As a result, they had seen all sorts of obscure teams play and had a large collection of souvenir caps.

"Why are they making you work on Christmas?" Mr. Callahan was asking him. "You worked on Thanksgiving."

"Well, they're giving me the twenty-third and Christmas Eve off, so at least I'll be able to spend a little time with all of you before I fly back," Uncle Steve said. "As long as I fly out early Christmas morning, I can make my shift."

"Can we go with you?" Gregory asked. "Please?" The last time they had gotten to fly in the plane had been way back in *October*.

"Yeah," Patricia agreed. "We could keep you company."

Mrs. Callahan looked up from her wonton soup. "You don't want to ride up with us?"

"Well — sure," Gregory said lamely, "but — " He stopped, and looked at Patricia.

"Planes are more fun than station wagons," she said.

Mr. and Mrs. Callahan exchanged glances.

"It seems to me that nice, loving children *like*

to ride with their parents," Mrs. Callahan said.

"While singing holiday tunes," Mr. Callahan added.

Patricia winced at the thought of that, and ate some of her broccoli instead of answering.

"Well, we'd be driving *home* with you," Gregory pointed out. "That counts, right?"

"Hey, if it's okay with all of you, it's fine with me," Uncle Steve said with a shrug.

"All right," Mrs. Callahan decided. "As long as I don't hear either of you arguing between now and Friday."

Gregory and Patricia looked at each other. "I would *never* fight with my best sister in the world," Gregory said.

"Your *only* sister," Patricia reminded him.

Gregory grinned at her. "Okay, but even if I had lots of others, *you'd* be the very best one."

"If I had nine brothers, you'd be in the top ten," Patricia retorted.

Gregory frowned, pretty sure that there was an insult in there somewhere. But his father was serving him some more rice and pork with garlic sauce, so he decided to pretend he hadn't heard her.

Then Patricia remembered something. "Oh," she said, and turned to Uncle Steve. "Is it okay if Santa Paws comes, too?"

Gregory promptly punched her in the arm. Patricia flinched and then socked him right back.

"Hey!" Mr. Callahan said sharply. "What did your mother just tell you two about fighting?"

"Patricia asked me to hit her the next time she said, 'Santa Paws,' " Gregory explained.

"Right, I forgot." Patricia tapped his shoulder where she had slugged him. "I withdraw my punch."

"Withdrawal accepted," Gregory said graciously, even though he was pretty sure he had a bruise.

"That wasn't a fight, he was just doing me a favor," Patricia told their parents. She was pretty sure *she* had a bruise, too.

Mr. and Mrs. Callahan looked suspicious, but they let it pass.

"Anyway," Uncle Steve said, "Santa Paws can come, as long as you bring his seat belt."

Gregory nodded. His mother had bought a special dog seat belt at the pet store. Santa Paws never wore it in the car, but he always wore it in Uncle Steve's plane. That way, there was no chance that he would jump around in the middle of the flight.

Then, just to make Patricia mad, Gregory reached over with his chopsticks and stole the last piece of sweet and sour pineapple from her plate.

"Greg!" she protested. "I was *saving* that."

Gregory ate the pineapple before she could steal it back. Then he plucked away a piece of her chicken, which he flipped to Santa Paws.

The dog caught the food with one quick lunge to his right, wagged his tail, and then sat politely on his rug again.

"Check your room *very carefully* before you go to sleep tonight," Patricia said in her most threatening voice.

Gregory shrugged. "Hey, no problem. When we get home, I'm going to spread all kinds of rumors about you on the Internet."

Patricia put her chopsticks down. "Oh, yeah? Well, *I'm* going to — "

Their mother frowned at them. "That sounds almost *exactly* like bickering to me."

Remembering that their plane trip hung in the balance, Gregory and Patricia instantly put on very sweet and innocent smiles.

"Never happen," Gregory assured her.

Patricia nodded. "Not us."

"*No way,*" Gregory said.

Two whole days of not arguing was going to be a challenge!

On Friday, school was only in session for a half-day and everyone was dismissed at eleven-thirty. Mrs. Callahan came to pick up Gregory and Patricia, and they went home to eat a quick lunch. Uncle Steve wanted to take off in the early afternoon, so that they would land before it got dark.

He kept his plane at a small airfield just over the New Hampshire border, and Mrs. Callahan drove them up there to meet him. Gregory and Patricia had each packed a small knapsack, and Gregory was also holding a picnic basket on his lap. Their parents would bring the rest of their stuff up to Vermont in the car. The plane was too small to carry bulky things like skis and heavy suitcases.

"I can't *wait* to go skiing," Gregory said, as they zipped along Route 95. "When're we going to go, Mom?"

Mrs. Callahan shrugged, and glanced in her rearview mirror. "I don't know. Monday or Tuesday, maybe?"

"*Cool*," Gregory said. He had asked for a new pair of ski goggles for Christmas, and he really hoped that he would get them. Either way, skiing was one of his favorite things to do.

"Can we go skating, too, Mom?" Patricia asked from the back. It had been so cold that the lake by the cabin was probably frozen by now.

"Sure," Mrs. Callahan promised. "If we're lucky, maybe we'll even be able to blast your father out of the house."

Gregory and Patricia laughed.

"Not likely," Patricia said.

"Never happen," Gregory agreed.

Feeling the holiday excitement in the air, the dog had trouble sitting still in the backseat. Gregory had given him a bath the night before, so his fur was nice and fluffy. Then Patricia had braided two red and green ribbons together and tied them around his neck in a big bow.

When they got to the airfield, Uncle Steve was busy filing his flight plan and running through a preflight checklist. It was really cold outside, so Gregory and Patricia waited in the car with their mother. Right before takeoff, they would give Santa Paws one last walk.

The runway had been plowed, of course, since the last snowstorm, and there was a huge pile of snow at the end of the tarmac. The small air-traffic control building had been shoveled out, but a lot of the small parked planes still had several inches of snow on their wing covers.

"Are you sure you two are dressed warmly enough?" Mrs. Callahan asked, looking worried. "You know how cold it gets up there."

"I have on like, *five* layers, Mom," Gregory said. With long underwear, a fleece turtleneck, and a hooded sweatshirt, plus a down vest under his ski jacket, he figured he was pretty well covered. He was also wearing a blue hat, a plaid wool scarf, his ski mittens, and a pair of heavy Gore-Tex lined hiking boots.

Mrs. Callahan turned around in her seat to

check on Patricia. "What about you? Are you going to be warm enough?"

Patricia was listening to her Walkman, and she lifted one of the headphones to one side. "What?"

"She wants to know if you're going to show off, and not zip your jacket and all," Gregory said.

Since they *were* going to Vermont, Patricia was wearing her Sorel winter boots, along with her Patriots jacket and ski gloves. She had also selected a pair of neon-yellow sunglasses to complete her ensemble. Other than that, she just had on a turtleneck and ragg wool sweater with her jeans.

"Where's your hat?" her mother asked.

Patricia looked down at herself. "I'm fine, Mom," she said. "I'm not cold."

Mrs. Callahan took off her own scarf. "Here, put this on. Where's your hat?"

Patricia checked the backseat, and then shrugged. "I don't know. I think I forgot it."

Mrs. Callahan sighed, and held out her own homemade knitted hat next.

"It's, um, nice and all," Patricia said politely. "But, um, well — it has a *pom-pom* on it."

Mrs. Callahan sighed again. "Humor me, Patricia. Okay? It's Christmas."

Reluctantly, Patricia tugged the hat on over her headphones. Pom-poms were *completely* not cool. Just in case they passed someone she knew, she slouched down in her seat so that her head was below the window.

Thinking that it might be the beginning of a game, the dog pawed her arm playfully.

"No, Santa Paws," Patricia said, and brushed his paw off. "*Sit*."

The dog sat.

"Good boy," she said, and then turned up the volume on her Walkman.

"Think you'll have enough to eat?" Mrs. Callahan asked.

Gregory grinned, and patted the heavy picnic basket. It was full of sandwiches, carrot sticks, homemade brownies, sodas, and juice boxes. There was also, of course, a small plastic bag full of Milk-Bones. "This'll hold us for *at least* an hour," he said.

Mrs. Callahan smiled, too. "All right, all right. I just can't help worrying." Then she pointed out through the windshield. "Okay, let's get ready. Here comes your uncle."

Before getting out of the car, Gregory reached for Santa Paws' harness. It snapped on around his chest and front legs, and then Gregory would adjust it to fit him just right. Once they were in the plane, he could thread the seat belt through the loop on the back of the harness. When that was done, Santa Paws would be safe in his seat for the rest of the flight.

"Extra large," Gregory said to him as he put on his leash. "Because you are a good, *big* dog."

The dog wagged his tail. Gregory thought he was good! He really didn't like the way the harness felt, but if Gregory wanted him to wear it, he would.

"Okay if I take him for a quick walk before we go?" Gregory asked his uncle.

Uncle Steve nodded, and checked his watch automatically. "Sure thing," he answered. He was wearing old army jungle fatigue pants, black work boots, an Oceanport PD cap, and a heavy-weight flight jacket. For warmth, he had added leather gloves, and a long striped scarf.

"Aren't you supposed to have on a bomber jacket and a white silk scarf?" Patricia asked.

Uncle Steve winked at her. "Fashion, I leave to *you*, my friend," he said. Then he lifted the picnic basket out of the front seat. "Weather looks great all the way up," he said to Mrs. Callahan.

Mrs. Callahan nodded. "That's good. We should get there by about nine tonight."

After walking along a stretch of bushes, Gregory brought Santa Paws back.

"Okay," he said cheerfully. "We're ready."

Mrs. Callahan hugged Patricia first, then Gregory, and finally, Santa Paws. "Okay, now be good," she said to all three of them. "Make sure you do everything your uncle tells you to do."

"Drop and give me twenty!" Uncle Steve said without missing a beat.

Gregory and Patricia both laughed, but didn't move.

Recognizing the *sound* of a command, if not the actual words, the dog sat down obediently and lifted his front paws in the air.

Uncle Steve bent down to pat him. "Good boy. At least someone's paying attention."

The dog barked. Uncle Steve thought he was good, too!

After saying one more good-bye to their mother, Gregory and Patricia crossed the airfield to the waiting plane. The Cessna was very snug, with just four seats inside. The outside of the plane was painted white, with red markings. There was a single propeller on the front, and the wings were attached to the top of the plane, instead of coming out from the sides. The landing gear was two fat rubber wheels at the bottom of the plane.

"Whose turn to sit up front?" Uncle Steve asked.

"Me!" Patricia said eagerly. Whoever sat up front would get the extra benefit of a little flying lesson. Uncle Steve always showed them how to use the rudder pedals to control the plane and let them steer for a minute. When they were old enough, he had promised that he would give them *real* lessons, and maybe they would be able to get pilot's licenses of their own.

Uncle Steve loaded their knapsacks and the picnic basket aboard and tied them down with rope. Then Gregory let Santa Paws into the back, and climbed in after him.

"Here you go, boy," he said, patting the seat on the right.

The dog woofed once, and bounced up onto the chair. Being in a plane was like riding in the car, but lots bumpier. He had flown with Gregory and Patricia before, and he knew what he was supposed to do. So he sat quietly, until Gregory attached his harness to the seat belt.

"Okay, good dog," he said. "Stay."

The dog wagged his tail, and then lounged back against the seat. Since they were still on the ground, he couldn't see much out through the window, but he could pretend.

Gregory reached into his jacket pocket. "Want a Milk-Bone?"

The dog tried to get up, but the seat belt kept him where he was. So he settled down and let Gregory hand the biscuit to him, instead.

Up front, Patricia was belting herself into the copilot's seat. In the meantime, Uncle Steve had put on his headset and was going through his final preflight check.

Gregory's favorite part of flying was when the

engine first started. The small cockpit would be filled with noise, and he could feel the whole plane seem to shake with excitement. It was usually too loud to talk when they were flying, but he enjoyed looking out the window so much that it didn't really matter.

Flying up to the lake cabin was always especially great, because the view of the mountains was *amazing* from the air. On a clear winter day like today, they would be able to take some really pretty pictures.

"Got plenty of gas?" Patricia asked.

Uncle Steve smiled and indicated the gas gauge. Then he twisted in his seat to check on Gregory and Santa Paws. "Everyone all set?" he asked.

Gregory and Patricia nodded, and the dog panted.

"Okay," Uncle Steve said. He gave them all a thumbs-up, and started the engine.

At first, the thundering noise always seemed deafening. But after a while, Gregory and Patricia would get used to it. The rumbling of the engine was so loud that they could feel it echoing inside their own chests. The propeller started off by spinning very slowly, but soon, it was whipping around so fast they almost couldn't see it anymore.

Once they were cleared for takeoff, Uncle

Steve taxied into position. They had to wait for a Piper Cub to take off, first.

When it was their turn to go, Uncle Steve gave them one final thumbs-up. Gregory and Patricia returned the signal enthusiastically.

Then they roared down the runway, picking up speed, until suddenly, they lifted off!

They were flying!

5

Gregory and Patricia peered out the windows as the plane banked to the right and climbed high into the sky. They watched all of the cars and buildings gradually get smaller and smaller, until even the broad stripes of interstate highways looked tiny.

After climbing up to their cruising altitude of about five thousand feet, Uncle Steve leveled the plane off.

"Do *not* feel free to move about the cabin!" he yelled over the noise of the engine.

Gregory and Patricia knew he was kidding, so they just grinned. Even if they had *wanted* to move around, there wasn't exactly much room.

Gregory reached over to pat Santa Paws and make sure he was all right. The dog licked his hand once, and then went back to gazing out the window at the clouds and bright blue sky.

"Do you think he likes it?" Gregory shouted to Patricia. "I can never tell!"

"He seems to, yeah!" she shouted back.

The dog looked alertly out the window, even though there wasn't much to see out there. But he wanted to be ready, just in case.

The flight was very smooth now, and Gregory opened the picnic basket to get them some snacks. There was a thermos of hot coffee, and he carefully poured out a cup and handed it up front to his uncle.

Uncle Steve nodded his thanks, but didn't say anything because he was busy talking into his headset.

Gregory passed Patricia a juice box and a tuna fish sandwich. Then he took a meat loaf sandwich and another juice box for himself.

Smelling the meat, the dog perked up. Gregory broke off part of his sandwich and fed it to him.

Soon, each of them — including Santa Paws — was eating a butterscotch brownie for dessert.

"These are *great!*" Uncle Steve yelled. "Remind me to tell your mother that!"

Gregory and Patricia nodded. They both really liked chocolate chip cookies, but these brownies were their favorite. On the other hand, even the *worst* cookies they had ever eaten had still been pretty good.

They were flying over the mountains now, and the wind had picked up. The turbulence made the plane jounce a little in the air, and Patricia grabbed the arm of her seat for a second before remembering that it wasn't cool to do things like that. She glanced back to see if Gregory had noticed. He was laughing, so she knew that he had.

For a while, they could see lots of small cities like Concord and Laconia, as well as wide, smooth highways. The mountains were covered with snow, and there were pine trees everywhere. If they had been on the ground, they would have been able to see other kinds of trees, but from the air, the mountains looked like one big Christmas tree farm.

As they flew further north, the landscape below them grew more beautiful and deserted. There were a few little towns in the White Mountain National Forest, but there were also miles and miles of wilderness.

The previous summer, they had hiked up Mount Monadnock in southern New Hampshire with their parents. It had been fun, but they got pretty tired. Other than that, the only time they ever made it to the tops of mountains was when they rode up on ski lifts. The Blue Hills in Massachusetts probably didn't count.

The White Mountains were really something, though. Tall, and craggy, and rugged. There were more clouds than there had been before, and they made the snow-covered mountains seem dark and mysterious.

"This is great!" Patricia yelled to Gregory.

"Yeah, I wish I remembered my camera!" he yelled back to her.

Then, all of a sudden, Uncle Steve tensed in his seat.

Patricia was the first one to notice. "Is anything wrong?" she asked.

He didn't answer, which *was* an answer.

The engine was beginning to cough and sputter, which got Gregory's attention. Before he could ask what was happening, the plane abruptly lost altitude and Uncle Steve had to fight the sluggish controls to keep them aloft.

They dropped again, and Gregory felt his stomach swooping down, too. There was a strong smell of burning electricity, and wisps of smoke floated out through the instrument panel.

Sensing the anxiety around him, the dog whined softly next to him. He wanted to stand up, but the seat belt held him in place.

Just as Uncle Steve started to call the emergency in, the engine died. In the sudden, shocking silence, they all stared at each other for a second.

"Okay, okay," Uncle Steve said. His face was pale, but he sounded very calm. "Okay." He stared at the instrument panel, and then made a few adjustments. "Okay." He tried to get the radio to work, but they were below the level of the mountains now, so it was mostly just static.

Seeing Patricia tighten her seat belt, Gregory quickly did the same. He also leaned over to make sure that Santa Paws was securely hooked up.

Uncle Steve did his best to smile at them. "I think we've got a little problem here, guys."

Gregory and Patricia looked at him with wide eyes. Santa Paws whined again, and Gregory put his hand out instinctively to pat him.

The plane sailed soundlessly through the air, but they were losing altitude very fast. Below them, there was nothing but mountains and endless forests.

"Are we crashing?" Gregory asked.

Patricia glared at him.

"I'm sorry," he said defensively. "I just wanted to know."

"Take the positions I taught you, okay?" Uncle Steve ordered, as he struggled to keep the plane in the air. "Keep your eyes closed, and don't look up until we come to a stop!"

There didn't seem to be any place to land, as the trees rushed closer and closer. One of the mountains had a small bald spot near the top, and Uncle Steve guided the unresponsive plane toward it.

They were falling, more than dropping, now.

Gregory and Patricia both bent forward in their seats, and covered their heads with their arms, trying not to scream in terror.

"Lie down, Santa Paws!" Gregory yelled without lifting his head. *"Lie down, boy!"*

They smashed down into the snowy clearing, but there wasn't enough room to stop. The landing gear collapsed on one side, and sent them sliding wildly out of control. The right wing slammed into a tree, and the force of the collision tore it right off the plane! They flipped over, and then spun backward across the snow. They spun around and around, crashing through bushes and snapping through small trees.

Finally, the plane came to a stop, and it was very, very still.

The dog was the first one to react. Hanging upside down made him feel panicky, and he yelped as he struggled frantically to get out of his harness.

Gregory opened his eyes, completely confused. Freezing cold air was rushing toward him from somewhere and a flailing paw scratched his face.

"Hey!" he protested, not sure where he was or why sharp claws had just raked across his cheek.

He couldn't understand why everything looked so strange, but then he realized that he was suspended upside down, that the plane had crashed, and — Patricia!

"Patty!" he shouted. "Uncle Steve! Are you okay?"

Neither of them were moving, and he could see that the windshield and instrument panel had been crushed. Were they all right? They *had* to be all right! Gregory gulped, feeling frantic tears fill his eyes.

"Patricia!" he shouted more loudly. "Uncle Steve! Wake up!"

Swinging helplessly next to him, the dog barked and yelped in a total frenzy of fear. What was happening? Why had they fallen out of the sky like that? He had mashed his side against the window, and it hurt a lot, so he yelped even more loudly.

"Santa Paws, no!" Gregory said. The terror was contagious, and he tried to fight it off. "*Shhh!* No! Good dog! *No!*"

Up in the front, Patricia groaned quietly.

"Patty, are you all right?" Gregory asked, trying not to cry. He could see that there was blood on her face, so she must be hurt. "Patty, wake up!"

He tore at his seat belt until he finally managed to unsnap the clasp. He landed hard on what would once have been the ceiling, and the plane lurched precariously to one side. Gregory was disoriented, but he made himself roll over until he was sitting upright.

Patricia's eyes opened partway, and she blinked a few times. Then she frowned at him.

"Why are you upside down?" she asked.

"*You're* upside down," Gregory said.

"Oh." She blinked again, her voice sounding strange and sluggish. "Why?"

Gregory started crying for real now, and it was hard to think. He rubbed his jacket sleeve across his eyes, and then forced himself to take a couple of deep breaths.

The skin of the plane had been torn open when the wing sheared off, and it was bitterly cold. Most of the fuselage — which was the metal body of the plane — on the right side was gone and the passenger's door was crumpled in.

"I-I don't — " Patricia was still blinking. "I'm not — " Suddenly, she figured out what was going on and her eyes flew open. "Greg! Are you okay?"

"I'm fine," he said shakily. Okay, she sounded like herself now. This wasn't as scary when she sounded like herself. "I'm coming up there to help you."

Patricia looked around, her expression much more alert now. "Wait. Calm the dog down first, he seems really upset."

The dog yelped and dug at the back of her seat with his paws. His side hurt! It hurt a whole lot! He was still caught in the seat belt and he desperately squirmed around, trying to get free.

"Come on, take it easy, boy," Gregory said, doing his best to stop him from struggling.

Patricia turned to check on Uncle Steve, who was unconscious. It was hard to tell exactly where he was injured, but blood was spreading down the front of his flight jacket. "Uncle Steve?" She put a trembling hand out to touch his shoulder. Then she gave it a gentle shake. "Are you okay? Uncle Steve?"

"Is he breathing?" Gregory asked.

"I don't know! I mean — " Patricia stopped for a second, so that she could calm down. "Yeah. I see his chest moving. I think he's really hurt, though."

Gregory got scratched on the face again, but then he wrapped his arms around Santa Paws to hold him still.

"It's okay, I've got you," he said soothingly. "Take it easy." He held his dog tightly, feeling both of their hearts pounding. Then he unhooked the seat belt and pulled it free of the harness.

Santa Paws fell on the roof of the plane with a loud thud and the plane lurched again. Landing that way made his shoulder hurt, too. He whimpered once, but then scrambled to his feet, and the plane swayed in response.

"Why's the plane moving?" Patricia asked uneasily.

Gregory shrugged. "I don't know. Maybe we're on some ice. Can you open your door?"

Patricia tried to pull the handle, and then made a tiny sound somewhere between a gasp and a moan.

"What?" Gregory asked, alarmed.

"I, uh, I must have banged my arm a little," she said, but her voice was so weak that Gregory knew she wasn't telling the whole truth.

"You're hurt," he said, "right?"

"I'm fine." Patricia gritted her teeth against the pain, and then bent to check the badly dented door. "I don't think it'll open, anyway. It's all smashed in."

The only thing Gregory knew for sure was that Patricia needed his help. "Good dog, stay," he said to Santa Paws. "I'm going to come up front now, Patty, okay?"

As he crawled toward her, the plane unexpectedly slid a few feet. He stopped, not sure why the plane was tilted on its side now, instead of being upside down. Then he lifted one hand to start forward again.

Patricia caught on first.

"Greg, don't move!" she shouted. "We're going to fall!"

He froze right where he was. "What?"

"I don't know where we landed," she said, "but — it's not good."

Well, no *kidding*. Their plane had crashed; of *course* it wasn't *good*. *None* of this was good.

"Don't anybody move!" Patricia said, her voice extremely crisp with authority. "Don't let Santa Paws move, either. I have to figure out what's going on here."

Outside, there was a distinct creaking sound, and the plane pitched forward again.

"What was that?" Gregory asked nervously.

"I don't know," Patricia said. "Just don't move."

She turned her head cautiously, looking in every direction. The plane seemed to be bobbing up and down, and she couldn't figure out why. When she squinted through what was left of the shattered windshield, she could see swaying tree branches and then — nothing at all. Empty air. Looking out through the cracked window in her door, she could see broken pine branches, snow — and more empty air.

"I think we're on top of a tree," she said slowly.

Gregory shook his head. "No, we're on the ground. We hit *way* too hard for it just to be a tree."

"Well, only the back part of it is on the ground then, because — " Then she sucked in her breath. "Oh, no."

They could hear more creaking, and what sounded like wood splintering. The plane bobbed

56

more, as though either the tail or the remaining wing was caught on something.

"What is it?" Gregory asked, his heart thumping in his ears.

Patricia took a deep breath, trying not to panic. "I think we're right on the edge of a mountain," she said.

6

Peering outside from his angle, Gregory saw that she was right, and that the front of the plane was suspended in midair. The only thing keeping them from falling over the cliff was a small fir tree. The tree was bent over from the weight of the plane, and he realized that the creaking sound was the trunk gradually breaking in half.

"It's okay, I can get you out," he said quickly. "I'm just going to reach over and — " As he leaned toward her, the plane lurched down another foot over the side of the mountain.

"Don't!" Patricia said.

Gregory edged back to where he had been, but the plane kept teetering.

"Just stay really still," Patricia said, her voice trembling. "If any weight shifts, we might — "

The dog stood up to see what was going on, and the plane teetered even more precariously.

"Don't!" Patricia said. "Make him sit!"

"*Sit*, Santa Paws," Gregory ordered, and then pressed down on his hindquarters.

Hearing the tension in his voice, Santa Paws quickly sat down. What was happening here? Gregory *never* got angry at him.

For the next minute, the only sounds were the wind whipping through what was left of the plane and the tree trunk creaking. Gregory and Patricia were both holding their breaths, too scared to budge.

"How high up are we?" he whispered.

Patricia was afraid to look again, so she didn't answer right away. "I don't know," she said finally. "Um, *high*, I think."

The plane swayed. The tree trunk creaked.

"Look," Gregory started. "If I — "

"Is the hole in the side big enough to crawl through?" Patricia asked.

The shell of the plane had been torn apart, so there was plenty of room. Most of the fuselage along the right side had been ripped away.

Gregory glanced over his shoulder. "Yeah. No problem. We can all fit."

There was more splintering, and the plane abruptly plunged down another foot. Patricia and Gregory gasped, and held their breaths again, as Santa Paws whimpered anxiously.

"Okay," Patricia said finally. "You and the dog get out."

Gregory stared at her. "What?!"

"Get out," she said, sounding very sure of herself. "Move as fast as you can."

"But — " Gregory stopped, and thought about it. Was that a good plan? Something didn't sound right to him. "No. That's a really bad idea."

The plane bobbed up and down. The tree trunk creaked. They might have minutes of safety left — or they might only have *seconds*.

"Just do it," Patricia said, so quietly that he could barely hear her. "Okay?"

Gregory shook his head. "*No.* If we do, there'll be way too much weight up front, and you'll fall."

"If you *don't*, *all* of us are going to fall," Patricia said through her teeth. "Just go, already!"

They stared at each other, Patricia still hanging awkwardly from her seat belt.

"You got a better idea?" she asked.

Suddenly, Gregory *did*.

"Yeah," he said, nodding. "How much does Uncle Steve weigh? Like, two hundred maybe?"

Patricia considered that. "Probably, yeah."

"And you weigh the least of any of us. So if we could get *him* out of the front, there'd be a whole lot more weight in the *back*, and we might be okay," Gregory said. "At least long enough to get us all out."

They stared at each other again.

"Well, I guess we can tell *your* mother's a physics teacher," Patricia said finally.

It was silent for a second, and then they both

laughed. *Feeble* laughs, but at least they were laughing.

"See if you can get your seat belt off, while I do his," Gregory suggested.

Patricia nodded, and fumbled awkwardly with the cold metal clasp. "He's going to be really heavy. Are you strong enough to pull him out?"

"*Santa Paws* is," Gregory said.

Hearing his name, the dog's ears pricked up.

Patricia nodded again. "You're right. Get some of the rope he used to tie our stuff down."

"Yeah." Then Gregory frowned. "Is it okay to move him? Maybe we're not supposed to. What if he hurt his back, or neck, or something? We could make it worse."

"It's okay," Patricia said. "I kind of think this counts as an emergency."

Well, that was true. If this wasn't an emergency, what *would* be? Gregory was having trouble unfastening their uncle's seat belt, and he finally realized that the metal part had been badly bent in the crash.

"What do I do? I can't open it, Patty," he said, hearing his voice shake. "We're going to fall, I *know* we are."

The plane kept bobbing up and down, and the tree kept creaking. Still too anxious to bark, the dog whined softly. First, he would sit, then he would get up, then he would sit down again. He knew that there were bad things happening here, and he wasn't sure how to help. So he just moved around skittishly in the back of the plane.

Patricia thought fast. "Go through his jacket pockets. Doesn't he have a Swiss Army knife?"

Gregory's hands were trembling so much that it was hard to make them work right. But he found the knife in the right side pocket and tugged it out. He chose the biggest blade and began hacking away at the thick seat belt.

He worked for a minute, but didn't make much progress. So he switched to one of the saw blades, yanking it back and forth as quickly as he could. He had expected Patricia to crawl over and help him once she got her seat belt off, but for some reason, she hadn't.

"You all right?" he asked over his shoulder.

"Unh-hunh," Patricia said without much expression in her voice. "Hurry up."

Was there something else wrong? She sounded like something else had gone wrong. *Everything* had gone wrong so far. But Gregory nodded and sawed even harder. When he had cut almost all the way through the seat belt, he paused.

"When I break through this, the weight's going to shift a bunch," he said tentatively.

"Unh-hunh," Patricia answered.

They both knew what might happen next, but there wasn't much they could do about it.

Gregory ripped through the last frayed

strands of the seat belt and Uncle Steve's body sagged limply into his arms. The unexpected weight was too much for him, and they both fell heavily onto what had been the ceiling.

In response, the plane swung violently to one side and then slipped forward another foot. More branches snapped off, and plummeted over the side of the cliff.

"Whatever we're going to do, we have to do *fast!*" Patricia yelled.

With his uncle's full weight crushing him, Gregory wasn't even sure if he could get up. Plus, he was so scared that —

"Don't think about it, Greg!" Patricia shouted from the front. *"Move!"*

A cold nose pressed against his cheek, and Gregory looked up at Santa Paws. The dog wagged his tail encouragingly, and then licked his face.

Okay, they all needed him to be brave right now — even Santa Paws. Gregory stretched his arm up toward what had been the floor of the plane and yanked on the first rope he saw.

The cargo underneath came tumbling down and the plane pitched forward again. There was the sound of more wood splintering, and then, a distinct *snap*. The plane sagged lower.

"Hurry!" Patricia said.

Gregory kicked the stuff out through the

shredded fuselage and shifted around until he could sit up. "Once I get him back here, you start climbing over, too, okay?" he said.

"Unh-hunh." Patricia gulped. "I mean, I'll try."

Gregory wrapped one end of the rope around Uncle Steve's chest and tied it tightly in a square knot, which was the only kind of knot he knew how to make.

"He's bleeding a lot, Patty," he said unsteadily.

"Go on!" she ordered.

Gregory nodded and pulled the rest of the rope through his hands until he got to the other end.

"Santa Paws?" he asked, looking around. "Come here, boy."

The dog wagged his tail gratefully and tried to climb onto his lap. He wasn't really sure what was going on, but they had never acted like this before. It was scaring him.

Gregory threaded the rope through the harness and tied another knot.

"Okay, Santa Paws," he said. "Go!"

The dog cocked his head to one side.

Gregory pushed him toward the hole in the fuselage. "Go on!"

The dog cocked his head the other way, perplexed.

Gregory yanked the rope, pretending that they were going to play tug-of-war. "Pull!"

Now, the dog understood. He knew the word

"pull." He grabbed the rope in his teeth and tugged as hard as he could. His legs were rigid, and he strained backward with all of his strength. His ribs were throbbing, but he just tugged harder.

"Good boy!" Gregory praised him. "Keep pulling!"

With the two of them working together, they were able to drag Uncle Steve over to the torn fuselage. Uncle Steve still wasn't conscious, but he was mumbling something Gregory couldn't quite hear. He thought he caught the words "call backup," but he wasn't sure.

"Pull, boy!" Gregory said again. "Good dog!"

The plane was still swaying back and forth, and more branches were snapping off.

When Uncle Steve was halfway outside to safety, Gregory turned to help his sister.

"Come on," he said, holding out his hand. "I'll pull you over."

She looked up at him, and he was shocked to see that she was crying. Patricia *never* cried.

"What?" he asked, afraid to hear the answer.

"I'm sorry," she said, crying harder. "My leg's stuck. I can't get it loose."

They were never going to get out. Never, never, never. Pretty much out of both courage and ideas, Gregory just stared back at her. Then he saw that from the knee down, her right leg was trapped underneath the smashed instrument panel. She was struggling to get free, but her leg was jammed there.

"Is it broken?" he asked.

Patricia shook her head, and rubbed some of the tears away with the side of her glove. "I don't think so. I'm just stuck."

Not sure what else to do, Gregory put his arms around her and pulled with all of his might.

Suddenly, the load in the back of the plane lightened and they pitched forward again. From his position, Gregory could see that there was a huge rocky ravine down below them. It went down at least two hundred feet, and — there was *no way* that they would survive, if they fell. And any second now, they might — he closed his eyes tightly and kept tugging.

"I'm sorry," Patricia kept saying, mainly to herself. "I'm really sorry."

"What if I get another rope?" Gregory asked. "Okay? I'll tie it around the back of the plane, and — "

There was a loud crack, and the plane plunged forward another couple of feet. Without looking, Gregory could tell that *most* of the plane was now hanging precariously over the edge of the cliff.

There was no time to lose!

"Santa Paws!" he bellowed.

Hearing his name, the dog sprang obediently

back inside the plane. Did they need his help? Whatever they wanted him to do, he was ready! Having his weight there made the nose of the plane rise a few inches.

"Okay, good dog. Stay," Gregory said, and crawled forward far enough to yank at the bottom of the instrument panel with his hands. "Maybe I can pry it up, and — "

Patricia shook her head. "I tried, it won't work. I don't think we can — " Then she stopped, her eyes brightening. "Oil! Get me some oil."

Gregory nodded and dug underneath the pilot's seat until he found a small plastic bottle of motor oil. He twisted the cap off, and handed it up to her.

Patricia shook the oil onto her jeans leg, forcing as much of the slippery liquid as she could below the instrument panel. Then she twisted back and forth, trying to get loose.

A few more branches broke, and they slid down another foot.

"It's not working," she said weakly. "I can't — "

No more time to fool around here — it was now, or never. "Close your eyes!" Gregory yelled. He snatched up the fire extinguisher that was also underneath the pilot's seat and sprayed the full contents at her leg. Then he threw the canister down and wrapped one arm around her. "Santa Paws! Come here!"

Instantly, the dog bounded over and Gregory grabbed onto his harness with his free hand.

"Pull, boy!" he shouted. "Go!"

The dog strained toward the torn fuselage, whimpering in frustration.

"Harder!" Gregory shouted, using his own legs to try and get them started. "Pull!"

Patricia gasped in pain, but then suddenly, her leg popped free and they all sprawled down in a heap.

"Come on!" Gregory said.

All three of them dove for the hole in the fuselage, scrambling out just as the fir tree finally gave way. The plane whipped past them, gathering speed until suddenly, it disappeared over the side of the mountain.

They had barely made it!

7

Gregory and Patricia lay in the snow, too exhausted to speak. After a minute, Patricia lifted herself up enough to look over the edge of the cliff, and then she sank back down. It was a *very* long drop.

"Is Uncle Steve okay?" she mumbled.

Gregory turned his head and saw their uncle's chest rising and falling as he breathed. He still seemed to be unconscious, though. "I think so," he answered. "He's breathing and everything."

They lay there for a few more seconds, in total silence, trying to catch their breaths. The snow was about a foot deep, and if they'd had enough energy, they would have been shivering. As it was, breathing in and out took all of their attention. Patricia didn't even have enough strength to worry about how badly her right arm hurt.

"We should have just driven up with Mom and Dad," Gregory said finally.

Patricia nodded. "Too bad we're not nice, loving children."

That broke the tension, and they snickered a little. Then they slumped back into the snow to rest some more.

Worried, the dog came over to check on them. They had never acted like this before! Why wouldn't they get up? Were they sick? This was scary! He sniffed Patricia's face, and then nudged Gregory's shoulder with his paw.

Gregory opened his eyes and lifted his hand to pat him. "It's okay," he said. "You're a good boy, Santa Paws."

That was more like it! Feeling better, the dog promptly turned in two circles and curled up between them in the snow. He rested his muzzle on Gregory's chest, and Gregory kept patting him. Patting his dog made it seem as though everything was going to be okay.

"If Santa Paws hadn't helped me pull, we wouldn't have gotten out in time," he said aloud.

"Yeah," Patricia agreed, and then paused. "You should give him a Milk-Bone."

The dog's ears flew up, and he looked at them hopefully.

It wasn't much of a reward, but Gregory fished around inside his jacket pocket until he found one. He gave it to Santa Paws, who wagged his tail and began crunching. Then Gregory stood up and looked around to see where they were.

There were craggy, tree-covered mountains in every direction. Mountains, mountains, and *more* mountains.

"Can you see any houses or anything?" Patricia asked.

Gregory shook his head. There were no signs of civilization at all. "I don't even see *roads*. We're in the like, *total* forest."

There had to be a town *someplace* nearby. It wasn't as though they'd crashed in the Yukon, right? "How about streetlights?" Patricia asked. "Or — I don't know — telephone poles, maybe."

Gregory looked and looked, but all he could see were mountains and trees. Hundreds and thousands and millions of *trees*. Dark, overcast sky. What might be a frozen lake off in the distance. Wherever they were, it looked as though they were on their own.

As though they were in *very* serious trouble.

Behind them, Uncle Steve started moving restlessly and saying something that sounded like "eltee." It didn't make any sense, but he seemed to be regaining consciousness.

Gregory hurried over to see if he was okay. Patricia followed him, wincing from the pain in her arm. The rope was still tied around their uncle's chest, and Gregory pulled it off.

Uncle Steve shifted his position, and then mumbled again.

"What's he saying?" Gregory asked. "L-T?"

Patricia shrugged as she took off her scarf and pressed it against the blood on his chest. Her right arm wouldn't work at all, so she had to do it one-handed. "I don't know," she said, trying to stop the bleeding. "Maybe he thinks this happened at work, and his lieutenant is here."

Gregory used *his* scarf to pick up a small handful of snow. Then he used the damp scarf to wipe the blood away from Uncle Steve's face. Most of it came right off, and he saw that it had all come from a cut on his forehead. The gash didn't seem to be very deep, but he would definitely need stitches. There was a huge, dark bruise there, too.

Washing his face with the cold snow must have helped, because Uncle Steve's eyes opened partway, and he squinted at them. He tried to sit up, then groaned and fell back down.

"Call backup," he whispered. Then his hand went down to where his holster would have been, if he was on duty. "Where's my service revolver?"

Gregory and Patricia looked at each other uneasily. Did he have amnesia, maybe? That would be really bad. He might even think they were perpetrators! If he suddenly started giving them their Miranda rights, it would just be too weird.

"Well — I think it's in Massachusetts," Gregory answered.

Uncle Steve looked confused. He tried to get up again, but then collapsed.

"I don't think you should try to move," Patricia said. "You might be really hurt."

Uncle Steve stared up at her in sudden recognition. "Patricia?" he asked in a dazed voice. "What happened? Are you all right?" He managed to lift himself onto one elbow, and then looked around anxiously. "Hey! Where's the plane?"

Gregory and Patricia shrugged and pointed over the edge of the mountain.

Uncle Steve's mouth dropped open. "What?! How did we get out?"

Patricia pointed at Gregory, and Gregory pointed at Santa Paws.

Uncle Steve's mouth stayed open, as he tried to take all of this in. Then he started shaking his head. "I can't believe I got you kids into this," he said softly. "I am *so* sorry."

"You should just lie down," Patricia advised. "I don't think it's good for you to be, you know, agitated."

Uncle Steve narrowed his eyes, trying to piece together what was going on. He might not have amnesia, but he still seemed pretty out of it.

"Because you're *hurt*," she elaborated.

Uncle Steve nodded, looking — even though he was an adult — a little overwhelmed for a second. Then he gave his head a shake and put on a more confident expression.

"Okay," he said, sounding very sure of himself. "Don't worry, everything's going to be okay." He tried to sit up all the way, and winced. Noticing the makeshift scarf-bandage, he raised one edge to look underneath.

"I think you maybe have a sucking chest wound," Patricia said uneasily. "Or — a pneumothorax."

Uncle Steve stared at her, and then, unexpectedly, he grinned. "Oh. You think so, Doc?"

Patricia looked a little offended, but then she grinned, too. She turned to Gregory. "Get a CBC, Chem seven, type and cross for two units, chest films, and hang a dopamine drip, *stat*," she said crisply.

Gregory looked at her suspiciously.

"Now!" she barked. "He's in v-tach!"

Instead of just grinning, Uncle Steve laughed outright when he heard that. "You know what? I think your sister watches too much television," he said to Gregory.

Gregory nodded. Sometimes Patricia even referred to herself as "Queen of the Remote Control." "Yeah," he agreed. "And she's like, in *love* with George Clooney."

Uncle Steve's face was tight with pain, but he laughed again. "Well, what would old George do in this situation?" he asked.

"Well — call nine one one, probably," Patricia said logically. "I mean, he's an *actor*." She paused. "That is, after he kissed me hello."

All three of them laughed this time.

The dog wagged his tail, because everyone seemed happy now. Things must be okay. Maybe they would go ride in the car soon. That's what they *usually* did after they got out of the plane. He didn't really know where the car *was* right now — but they would know. They *always* knew. So he sat down in the snow to wait, watching them alertly.

"Don't worry," Uncle Steve said to Patricia. "I think it's just my collarbone. Looks like a compound fracture, that's all." He took a deep breath and started to sit up all the way, but then his face paled.

Patricia looked scared. "What?"

"And maybe my hip," he said in a faint voice. He tried to move again, and then sucked in his breath. "Oh, boy." He smiled feebly at them. "I, uh, might've wrenched my back a little, too."

Patricia and Gregory exchanged nervous glances.

"What do we do?" Gregory asked.

"Let me think for a minute, okay?" Uncle Steve said, speaking with an effort.

Gregory and Patricia waited nervously for him to open his eyes again. The dog moved into a worried crouch, since they all seemed to be up-

75

set again. He whimpered once, and Gregory automatically patted him.

"Okay," Uncle Steve said finally. His voice sounded a *little* stronger, but not much. "First things, first. Are either of you hurt?"

Gregory shook his head, but Patricia didn't answer.

"Patricia?" Uncle Steve asked more firmly.

"I kind of banged my arm," she muttered.

Since her right arm was just hanging uselessly at her side, it was pretty obvious that she had broken something.

"Okay," Uncle Steve said gently. "We're going to get a splint on you as soon as we can, and — it'll be okay. How bad's the pain?"

Patricia shrugged, avoiding his eyes.

"Okay," Uncle Steve said. "I hear you." He let out his breath. "Did either of you turn on the ELT?"

The ELT was the Emergency Locator Transmitter, which looked sort of like a walkie-talkie. ELTs sent out emergency signals, so that rescue planes would be able to find downed aircraft easily. And — they hadn't turned it on. In fact, neither of them had even *thought* of it. They had just assumed he meant "lieutenant." Patricia and Gregory both ducked their heads and looked guilty.

"Okay, no problem. Don't worry about it," Uncle Steve said calmly. He pulled in a deep breath.

"Where's the survival pack? I've got a handheld one in there."

Patricia and Gregory looked even more guilty. Then Gregory pointed miserably over the side of the mountain. After all of the times they had flown in the plane, the one time there was a *real* emergency, they hadn't remembered what to do. And now, it might cost them their lives.

Uncle Steve closed his eyes briefly, but then gave them a reassuring smile. "Okay. No problem," he said again. "I had to go a little off-course to get us down, but I filed a flight plan, so they'll know where to start looking. It just might take a little while."

"Will they be here today?" Gregory asked.

Uncle Steve glanced up at the sky. Ominous grey clouds had rolled in, and it was starting to get dark. "Probably in the morning," he answered.

So they were going to have to spend the night out here, alone, in the middle of the wilderness, in *December*.

"We're going to die," Gregory said grimly, "right?"

That was the *last* thing Patricia felt like hearing, and she couldn't help giving him a little shove.

Uncle Steve shook his head. "We are *not* going to die. We're going to stay really calm, set up some kind of shelter, and get a fire going. Okay?"

Thinking about sitting in front of a warm fire, Gregory and Patricia suddenly realized that their teeth were chattering. It was very windy on the mountain, and even Santa Paws seemed to be shivering.

"We'll all feel a lot better once we get warm," Uncle Steve promised.

At the moment, neither Gregory nor Patricia could imagine how they could feel much *worse*.

"I'm really sorry about the survival stuff," Gregory said. "I — I just forgot, I — "

Patricia interrupted him. "*I* should have remembered. I'm older than he is."

"And *I* should have figured out a way to land in the middle of some nice little town common somewhere," Uncle Steve said. "Look, we all got out of the plane in one piece, right? *That's* what's important."

"Yeah, but — " Patricia started.

"It's going to be dark soon," Uncle Steve said, cutting her off. "We need to move quickly here. Greg, take the dog, and go see how much firewood you can find." He looked around the mountain face, and then pointed to a spot surrounded by a thicket of pine trees. "See where those rocks are? And that fallen tree? That's where we'll settle in. We should be protected from the wind up there."

Gregory nodded, and climbed stiffly to his feet.

"Come on, Santa Paws," he said, giving him a short whistle.

The dog jumped up, relieved to be *doing* something. Maybe *now* they would go to the car. Sitting here in the wind was just too cold.

Patricia and Uncle Steve watched as Gregory and Santa Paws went trudging off through the foot-deep snow.

"So," Uncle Steve said wryly. "We having fun yet?"

Patricia tried to smile.

So far, her Christmas vacation had been anything but *fun*.

8

Patricia knew she should be doing something constructive, but she was too tired to think. It was easier just to rest for another minute. Uncle Steve looked even worse than she felt, but he motioned her over.

"Come here, honey, and let me look at you for a minute," he said.

Patricia got up, and moved to him. Uncle Steve held her chin gently so he could examine her face. Then he picked up the scarf Gregory had dropped, and used the end to blot away the blood below her nose and on her chin.

"Did you bite your lip?" he asked.

Patricia thought back, and then nodded. "When we crashed, I think."

"Okay," he said, and dabbed lightly at the cut. "You went right through. It looks like you had a little nosebleed, too. Do your teeth feel okay?"

Patricia ran her tongue around the inside of

her mouth to be sure, and then nodded. None of them seemed to be loose or anything.

"How about your head?" Uncle Steve asked, looking concerned. "Do you think you hit it?"

"Well — it doesn't hurt," Patricia said uncertainly.

"Good." Uncle Steve rolled some snow into the scarf, and then handed it to her. "Hold that against your lip, and let's see if we can get some of the swelling down."

Patricia nodded, and pressed the snow on the spot that hurt the most. "Do you think *you* have a concussion?" she asked, her voice muffled by the scarf.

"Who, me?" he asked cheerfully. "This is nothing. I used to play *football*, remember?" Then he indicated a couple of objects half-buried in the snow. "What're those?"

Patricia went over to see, surprised to find herself limping. Apparently, she had twisted her knee while trying to get free from the instrument panel. It hurt, but not nearly as much as her arm did. She bent down on her uninjured leg to examine the things that must have been knocked out of the plane during all of the confusion.

"My knapsack," she said. "And — I think this might be a life jacket."

Uncle Steve's eyes lit up. "*Good.* I've got some

MREs, and I forget what else, wrapped up in there."

MREs were Meals-Ready-to-Eat, which were Army rations. Patricia had never had one before, but *anything* would taste good right now. She was starting to get really hungry. Just in case, she kept poking through the snow with the toe of her oil-and-foam-stained boot to see what else she might find. Her knee felt swollen and clumsy, but she could still bend it a little.

"I see some stuff from the picnic basket, too," she said. "There's a Coke, and — I see the brownies!"

Uncle Steve nodded. *"Outstanding.* See if you can get all of it piled together, and then when Gregory gets back, he can carry everything."

While she was doing that, Uncle Steve dragged himself over to the edge of the cliff. It must have hurt a lot, because he groaned a few times, but he would just grit his teeth and keep going.

He studied the broken fir tree, and shook his head. "Was the plane caught on this?"

Patricia nodded.

Uncle Steve nodded, too, before shaking his head again. Then he peered down into the deep gorge. There was a sheer rock face on both sides, and the whole thing was coated with ice and snow. He stared at the wreckage down on the rocks, and then let out his breath.

"How close did we come to going over?" he asked.

Really close. "Um, about a second and a half," Patricia said.

Uncle Steve let out a low whistle.

Patricia glanced behind her to make sure that Gregory hadn't come back yet. "I, um, I pretty much panicked," she confessed. "I thought I was maybe even going to throw up or something. But Greg was *really* brave."

"I'm guessing you did fine," Uncle Steve said, and stared at the battered wreckage some more. "In fact, you kids are really something."

Patricia shrugged self-consciously. The only thing she could remember was how terrified she had been, every single second. Just being *scared* — which was how she felt right now — was definitely an improvement. "Do you think we can climb down there, and maybe get the ELT and all?" she asked.

Uncle Steve looked at her incredulously. "I don't think a team of fully-equipped *paratroopers* could climb down there," he answered.

Patricia nodded, and then couldn't help shivering. A couple of seconds either way, and she would have fallen onto those rocks. It made her dizzy to look down there, so she concentrated on gathering up the stray cargo, instead.

Across the clearing, Gregory was stomping around near the fallen tree with a huge armload of wood. He saw them watching, waved, and hiked back over. Santa Paws galloped playfully next to him, barking every so often.

Gregory's face was red from all of the exercise, but he was smiling. "There's a whole *bunch* of wood over there," he said. "Dead trees, and all. We found most of the wing, too. Can we maybe use it like a sled for you, Uncle Steve?"

"Let me see if I can get over there by myself, first," Uncle Steve suggested. "Then we'll use it to help build a shelter."

"Okay," Gregory said, sounding remarkably chipper. "We'll go get it. Come on, boy!" he called to Santa Paws, and they headed off again.

"Why don't you carry what you can," Uncle Steve said to Patricia, "and I'll catch up."

Patricia nodded and unzipped her knapsack. There was just enough room inside to pack in the few things she had found from the picnic basket. When she came across the plastic bag of carrot sticks her mother had cut up for them, she had to stop for a second so she wouldn't cry.

Did their parents know what had happened yet? Were they upset? What if she never saw them again? She squeezed her eyes shut and tried to remember the last thing she had said to both of them.

Her mother had been worried that she hadn't dressed warmly enough for the trip. And — her mother was *right*. Her father had stayed back at the house, because he was waiting for some overnight mail to come from New York. But he had given each of them a big hug before they left, the best kind where he lifted them right off the ground and spun around a couple of times.

"You all right?" Uncle Steve asked.

Patricia nodded and swung the knapsack over her good arm. That way, she could also carry the rolled-up life jacket in her hand and only have to make one trip. Then she started limping toward the rocks.

Watching Uncle Steve drag himself inch by inch through the snow made her want to cry all over again. His jaw was very tight, and he kept his eyes closed most of the time. He was breathing really hard, and every few feet, he would groan softly and suck in his breath.

"Um, maybe we *should* make a sled," she said hesitantly.

For a second, she thought he was going to yell at her. But then, he just shook his head.

"I'm fine," he panted. "Okay? It's just going to be slow."

Patricia nodded. Her father was always talking about how incredibly stubborn his little brother Steve was — and so, she wasn't about to argue. And, hey, *she* had been accused of being pretty stubborn, too.

About fifty feet away, she could see that Gregory had managed to tie the rope to the sheared-off wing. Now he and Santa Paws were pulling it toward them like an ungainly pair of Santa's reindeer.

A large branch was poking up out of the snow, and Uncle Steve paused long enough to tear off a thick twig. He stuck it between his teeth, and bit down *hard*. Then he resumed crawling. He had only made it about ten more feet, when Gregory and Santa Paws got to them.

"Taxi!" Gregory announced brightly.

Uncle Steve hesitated, but then gave up. Slowly, he eased himself up onto the metal wing. Once he was aboard, Gregory tugged on the rope, but the improvised sled didn't move.

"We pulled him before," he said to Santa Paws, "remember? We can do it again."

The dog cocked his head.

"*Pull*, boy," Gregory said. Then he yanked on the rope, using all of his weight.

Santa Paws joined in, ignoring the pain in his side, but it still didn't budge.

Uncle Steve swung his uninjured leg over the side and pushed powerfully against the snow. With that extra effort, the wing-sled squirted forward. Using the momentum, Gregory and Santa Paws started pulling the wing-sled across the drifts.

It seemed to take forever, but finally they all made it over to the fallen tree. Patricia and

Gregory sat heavily on top of a rock, while Uncle Steve stayed right where he was, trying to catch his breath. Even Santa Paws looked tired. It was dusk now, and they had to squint through the shadows to see each other.

Uncle Steve broke the silence. "Thanks, guys. Sorry to be so much trouble." He slid himself off the wing, his face grey from exhaustion and pain. "Greg, if you can lift the wide end up on the tree, and the other side onto that rock, we'll be in business."

"I can help," Patricia offered.

Uncle Steve shook his head. "No, why don't you get some more wood, while it's still light enough to see. But *don't go out of sight.*" Then he felt around inside his right jacket pocket and frowned.

"Oh," Gregory said, and reached into his own pocket for the Swiss Army knife. "Are you looking for this?"

Uncle Steve nodded. "Thanks."

While Patricia gathered wood, and Gregory worked on the shelter, Uncle Steve began to cut pine boughs from some of the nearby trees with his good arm. Normally, of course, he would never have damaged trees that way — but, this wasn't exactly a normal situation. When survival was at stake, the rules changed.

For lack of a better idea, the dog followed Patricia around. He liked to carry things in his mouth, so when Patricia gave him a stick, he happily took it. She kept going back and forth with single armloads of kindling and thicker sticks. Each time, he would dance along next to her.

"Are you a good boy?" she asked him.

The dog barked, which made the stick fall out of his mouth. He grabbed it back up and shook his head playfully from side to side. If he was lucky, maybe she would throw it for him! Just because his ribs hurt, didn't mean that he couldn't still have fun!

"No, not now," Patricia said. Her hands and feet were so cold, and her arm was throbbing so much that the *last* thing she felt like doing was playing fetch. Besides that, her knee was beginning to ache more than ever. "Leave me alone, Santa Paws!"

The dog lowered his ears and stopped wagging his tail. Then he dropped the stick into the snow. Did she think he was a bad dog? She *must*.

Patricia sighed, ashamed of herself for having shouted at him. After all, only about an hour ago, he had helped save her *life*. "I'm sorry, you're very good, Santa Paws," she apologized. "It's just — right now, we have to work."

The dog still kept his head down, with his tail between his legs. He must have done *something* wrong, but he didn't know what it was. Now his side hurt even more than it had before.

Seeing him upset was more than she could take, and Patricia felt tears start down her cheeks. She let the sticks she was clutching fall, and then she sat down in the snow. It was cold, but she didn't care. She was *already* so cold that she couldn't think straight, anyway.

Her arm hurt so much that it felt like it was on fire. She hunched over it, rocking slightly. Gregory and Uncle Steve — and Santa Paws — were so brave, and she just wasn't making it, here. She buried her face in her sleeve and cried as quietly as she could. If they heard her, or came to look for her, she would feel even worse.

The dog *couldn't stand it* when he saw anyone cry. He hated it when people were sad. Especially *his* people. He sat down and nuzzled up next to her, trying to get as close as he could.

Patricia put her arm around him and hugged him tightly. His fur felt warm, and comforting. She had never been outside in the forest like this before, and she couldn't believe how *dark* it was. How frightening it seemed. The clouds were so thick that there weren't even any stars out.

Then she heard Gregory calling her name, his voice sharp with fear.

"Patricia!" he yelled. "Patricia, where are you?"

Santa Paws was already on his feet. Patricia hung onto his collar to help herself stand up faster. Then she stumbled through the snow in the direction of her brother's voice.

"What's wrong? I'm over here!" she yelled back.

"Come quick!" he said, sounding frantic. "I need help!"

9

It was hard to see in the dark, but Santa Paws was galloping ahead of her. Patricia just kept watching for a moving shape, and then she would race after it.

Then she ran into Gregory — *literally* — at the edge of the clearing.

"What's wrong?" she asked, out of breath. "Are you hurt?"

"Uncle Steve fainted or something," Gregory said, sounding very close to tears. "He was helping me make a fire pit, and then he just passed out. I didn't know what to do!"

Patricia put her hand on his shoulder to calm him down. "Just show me where he is, okay?"

Gregory nodded, and motioned for her to follow him.

When they got to the shelter, Patricia saw that Uncle Steve was lying on his back in the snow. She crouched down next to him, peering through the darkness. His breathing seemed nice and steady, but he was definitely unconscious.

"*Fix* him," Gregory said urgently. "I mean, you know all that medical stuff."

Patricia sighed. "I just know a bunch of words, Greg — I don't know how to *do* anything."

He stared at her accusingly. "But — I thought you *knew* stuff. You always act like you know *everything*."

"Give me a break, I'm only *twelve*!" she said.

They glared at each other until Patricia finally took a deep breath.

"Look," she said. "We're really cold, and we're really scared, and we don't know how to help him. Let's try to be nice to each other, okay?"

"Be sweet," Gregory muttered.

Patricia smiled a little. That was what their grandmother always said to them right before she hung up the telephone, instead of "goodbye." "Yeah," she said. "Exactly."

Watching them, the dog paced anxiously and whined deep in his throat.

Patricia slipped her glove off and tapped her uncle's face lightly with her hand. "Uncle Steve?" she asked tentatively.

There was no response.

Gregory and Santa Paws were waiting for her to make everything all right, so she tapped his face again. Then she nudged his arm.

Finally, his eyes opened. He shook his head to

clear it, squinted at them, and then sat up partway.

"Sorry," he said hoarsely. "Got a little dizzy there." He rubbed his hand across his eyes and shook his head a few more times. "Okay." He frowned when he noticed Patricia's bare hand. "Hey, put your gloves on — it's cold out here."

If he was being authoritative, he must be okay. Or *better*, anyway. Patricia awkwardly wormed her hand back inside her glove. Just a couple of minutes of being exposed to the cold air had numbed her fingers pretty badly.

"Take it easy, I'm all right," Uncle Steve said to Gregory. "I overdid the lifting, that's all."

"You have to be careful," Gregory answered shakily. "That was way too scary."

Uncle Steve nodded. "I know. I'm sorry, pal."

While they were talking, Patricia glanced around the campsite. From what she could see, they had made a lot of progress. The wing was resting across the big tree trunk and a gigantic boulder to form the roof of a primitive triangular shelter. Someone — Gregory, presumably — had built up a snow wall to fill the open spot in the back. As a result, the shelter was fully enclosed, except for a wide opening in the front.

The snow had been trampled down to make a hard surface. Cushiony pine branches lined the bottom of the shelter to insulate it from the snow. In front of the opening, there was a neat semicircle made out of fairly big rocks and some jagged pieces of aluminum from the wing. They would form a firebreak. It would block the wind from the fire, and it would also help reflect the heat into their lean-to.

Smaller rocks were arranged together in front of the firebreak, as a base for their campfire. Otherwise, the heat from the coals would just melt all of the surrounding snow and the fire would go out right away.

"This is really *good*," Patricia said admiringly. "You're like, *nature guys*."

Uncle Steve's teeth flashed, so he must have smiled.

Gregory raised his fist in the air. "Airborne!" he said, trying to make his voice deep. Sometimes, he and his friend Oscar liked to pretend that they were in the Army, and they were always trying to chant infantry cadences.

"Okay, Airborne Ranger," Uncle Steve said, still smiling. "See if you can rip one more piece of metal off the end of the wing. We'll build the fire on it."

Gregory nodded, and climbed up on top of the fallen tree to work on the wing.

Uncle Steve shifted his position to one side and reached inside his jacket. His movements were extremely cautious. Finally, he came out with a small penlight. He flicked it on, and the bright beam cut through the darkness.

Now that they could see better, they all visibly relaxed. The campsite seemed friendlier, somehow. The black expanses of the wilderness were still surrounding them, but it felt as though they were in a safe haven.

Next, Uncle Steve dug painfully into one of the bellows pockets on his pants leg. He pulled out an ordinary plastic trash bag and then sliced open the two long sides with his Swiss Army knife.

"Here," he said, and handed it to Patricia. "Spread it out on the floor of the shelter. It'll help us stay dry."

Patricia nodded and carried the bag inside the shelter. Gregory had managed to tear another piece of fuselage from the wing, and he set it down on the bed of rocks.

Since everyone else had something to do, the dog looked at Uncle Steve expectantly.

"Santa Paws, why don't you just wag your tail and keep up morale?" Uncle Steve suggested.

The dog promptly lifted his right paw.

"Okay," Uncle Steve said agreeably. "That's good, too." Then he retrieved another garbage bag from his pocket. "Lay this one out on the ground, Patricia, and then we can inventory our supplies. And Greg, can you help me clear out my pockets?"

Gregory hesitated. "Will I hurt you?"

"No," Uncle Steve said, although it probably

wasn't true. "I just can't get to the ones on the left side very well."

Patricia watched as the two of them pulled out a surprising variety of objects. Between the flight jacket and the army pants, Uncle Steve had an *amazing* number of pockets.

"Are you maybe Mary Poppins in disguise?" she asked.

Uncle Steve nodded ironically. "Oh, yeah. I'm practically perfect in every way." He fumbled through the pile one-handed until he found a small plastic container of waterproof matches and a tube of fire-starter. "Here we go, Greg — it's show time."

Soon, a small blaze was glowing on the piece of fuselage. Following their uncle's instructions, Gregory carefully surrounded it with more kindling. Then, once the fire had caught pretty well, he added some thicker sticks. The wood crackled and snapped, and burned noisily away.

They all, including Santa Paws, gathered around the fire. No one spoke, so that they could just enjoy the luxury of starting to feel warm again. Or, at least, not quite as *cold.*

"Let's break out the brownies," Uncle Steve said finally. "I think we could all use a snack."

Patricia looked inside her knapsack until she found the foil-wrapped package. While she was at it, she took out the rest of the things from the picnic basket. There was a squashed meat loaf sandwich, the bag of carrot sticks, a can of Coke, a package of Santa Claus cocktail napkins, and a juice box. It might not be much, but it *seemed* like great riches.

There were six brownies in the package, and they each had one. Santa Paws gulped his down in one swallow, but the rest of them took their time. They wanted to savor every single bite. In the end, of course, Gregory ended up sharing the rest of his with Santa Paws, anyway.

"What else have you got in there?" Uncle Steve asked, indicating the knapsack.

"I don't know," Patricia said, and then she flushed self-consciously. *"Vogue."*

Uncle Steve grinned. "Well, see," he said to Gregory, "things were looking mighty bleak, but now we're going to be able to sit here, and get up-to-speed on the spring collections. Life is *good.*"

The thought of them all sprawling in front of the fire, reading *Vogue*, was a pretty funny image, and Gregory laughed.

"I didn't know we were going to crash," Patricia said defensively. "So I just brought vacation stuff."

Gregory started pulling things out of the knapsack. His face lit up when he saw her notebook computer.

"Hey, whoa!" he said eagerly. "We can send *E-mail*! Then they'll come rescue us!"

Uncle Steve and Patricia just looked at him.

"It'll be great," Gregory went on. "I'll send some to Gram, and to Oscar, and — " He stopped. "Why aren't you guys happy?"

Patricia moved her jaw. "I'm going to say one word to you, Gregory."

"Plastics?" Uncle Steve guessed.

Patricia and Gregory looked at him, perplexed. He shook his head. "Never mind."

Patricia focused on Gregory. "*Modem*," she said. "The word is *modem*."

Gregory's face fell. "Oh. Right." To use the modem, they needed access to a telephone line — and if they were near a telephone, they could just *call* for help.

"It was a good thought, though," Uncle Steve said kindly.

"Or we could just describe it as . . . a *thought*," Patricia said, and winked at Gregory.

After unloading the knapsack, Gregory emptied his own pockets. He also helped Patricia with hers, since she couldn't move her arm very well. Then he unstrapped the bright orange life jacket. Two dark brown sealed bags fell out, along with a metal cup with a sturdy handle and a cylinder that looked like a firecracker.

"What's that?" Patricia asked.

"It's a flare," Uncle Steve answered. "We can use it for a signal, if someone flies over. Greg, slice each of the MREs at one end, and we'll see what we have."

The two Meals-Ready-to-Eat had vacuum-sealed food packets inside. Some of the packets were pliable, and the others seemed to be shrink-wrapped. The first meal was corned beef hash, with a pack of dry fruit mix. There was also an oatmeal cookie bar, crackers, a packet of apple jelly, a brown plastic spoon, an envelope of cocoa powder, and some Beverage Base powder — which was like Tang or Kool-Aid. There was also something called Accessory Packet A. It contained two Chiclets, water-resistant matches, a tiny bottle of Tabasco sauce, a Wet-Nap for washing, some tissues, coffee, sugar, salt, and cream substitute.

The other meal was very much the same, except that the main course was escalloped potatoes with ham, and it had a chocolate covered brownie, some applesauce, and a package of caramels to go along with its accessory packet.

"Fill the two bags with snow, and put them near the fire," Uncle Steve said. "Close enough so it'll start melting. Then we'll be able to heat up some water for cocoa."

It turned out that Uncle Steve had been carrying all sorts of useful things in his many pockets. There was an emergency space blanket, a squat white candle, a black watch cap, some

Chap Stick, his wallet, car keys, some stamps, a half-eaten roll of Tums, and a box of cough drops. He had also unearthed a nail clipper, a handkerchief, a notepad, two pens, another garbage bag, two packages of pocket heaters, needle-nose pliers, a roll of duct tape, and — of course — his Swiss Army knife.

"Adults have a lot of baggage, huh?" Patricia remarked.

"So I hear," Uncle Steve said dryly.

Along with *Vogue*, Patricia had brought the latest issue of *Entertainment Weekly*, the most recent J. Crew catalog, and a copy of *Wuthering Heights*. She had also packed extra sunglasses, her Walkman, some cassettes, her favorite pink sweatshirt, a Magic Marker, a hairbrush, some Lauren perfume, a blue ponytail holder, and vanilla-flavored lip gloss.

"It's good to look and smell your best when you're in a plane crash," Uncle Steve observed.

"Uh-huh," Patricia said. Dryly.

The only things Gregory had in his pockets were six more Milk-Bones, forty-two cents, half a candy cane, a cheap harmonica he didn't know how to play, an old ticket stub from a Bruins game, some sea shells, and a battered tennis ball.

Santa Paws had been overjoyed to see the tennis ball — to say nothing of the Milk-Bones.

Gregory shook his head. "Not now," he told

him as he zipped them back into his jacket pocket. "Maybe later."

Disappointed, the dog flopped back down by the fire. So Gregory relented and gave him a small piece of Milk-Bone. The dog wagged his tail and started crunching.

"Are you warm enough now to take your jacket off for a minute?" Uncle Steve asked Patricia. "I want Gregory to put a splint on that arm."

Patricia nodded, and awkwardly unzipped it. She was able to slip the jacket off her left side with no trouble, but the right side was a different story. The second she jarred her arm, she gasped and her eyes filled with tears.

Hearing the distress in her voice, the dog scrambled up. He watched her intently, his forehead furrowed with worry. He had never felt so helpless before!

"Okay, okay," Uncle Steve said quickly. "Greg's just going to ease it off for you. Hold my hand, and squeeze as hard as you want, okay?"

Patricia held his good hand with *her* good hand.

Gregory slowly peeled her jacket off. He *really* didn't want to hurt her. His sister had her eyes shut the whole time, but he could feel that she was shaking.

"You want to wear my down vest?" he asked.

"I've got way more layers on than you."

Patricia opened her eyes. "Won't you be cold?"

"Not as cold as *you* are," Gregory said. He took off his jacket, and unsnapped the down vest he was wearing underneath. Then he guided the right side over her broken arm, and helped her stick her left arm in, too. It was terrible to see her shivering so much, and he quickly fastened all of the snaps.

"From now on, long underwear," Patricia vowed. "Even in August."

Gregory had to laugh as he pictured her lounging on Crane's Beach in her bathing suit, sunglasses — and long underwear.

"Take her glove off, and feel her hand," Uncle Steve said, "I want to make sure she's getting enough circulation."

"It's nice and warm," Gregory reported.

"Now press one of her fingernails and release it," Uncle Steve told him.

"Her nail turned white, and then back to pink."

"Good. Now cut *Vogue* in half," Uncle Steve said. "Just go right down the binding. Then hold the pieces against her other arm to see if they'll fit. I think they're going to be too long, so you can just cut them down to size."

The magazine *was* too long, and Gregory sawed about three inches off. He rolled one half around her upper arm and taped it in place with some of the duct tape. Then he did the same thing to her forearm. He had to be very careful with the tape, so that the splints wouldn't be too tight.

The last step was making a sling. First, he wrapped his scarf just below her elbow, and then tied it around her neck. After that, he looped his belt around her wrist and fastened it around her neck, too. The most important part was for her wrist to be higher than her elbow. Gregory turned the penlight back on, and flashed it up and down her arm to make sure everything looked okay.

Patricia kept her eyes closed and held onto Uncle Steve's hand the whole time.

"How does it feel?" Uncle Steve asked.

Patricia managed a weak smile. "Like I have a broken arm."

Uncle Steve nodded, and gave her hand a sympathetic squeeze. "You did a good job, Greg," he said.

Gregory zipped her jacket back up, trying not to jostle her arm. Patricia mouthed the word, "Thanks," and he nodded.

Now it was Uncle Steve's turn!

10

U ncle Steve was so badly hurt that there
wasn't really very much that Gregory could
do to help him. They didn't have any bandages,
so he pressed the whole package of Santa Claus
cocktail napkins against the torn part of his
shoulder. Then he tied it in place with Patricia's
scarf and used Uncle Steve's belt for a sling.

Splinting his broken hip was even more complicated. Gregory searched through their woodpile until he found a stick long enough to reach
from the outside of his uncle's ankle, all the way
up to his rib cage. Then he selected another one
to fit against the inside of his leg.

Next, he sliced the sleeves off Patricia's pink
sweatshirt and set them aside. The Swiss Army
knife was pretty much worth its weight in *gold*.
After that, he cut the body of the sweatshirt into
two pieces. He rolled each piece around one of
the sticks for padding and started lightly taping
them into place.

"Is that too tight?" he asked nervously.

Uncle Steve shook his head, gritting his teeth against the pain.

Gregory taped the two sticks, so that Uncle Steve's hip was immobilized as much as possible. Then he rezipped his flight jacket and tied his scarf for him. Finally, he used the Swiss Army knife to cut the discarded sweatshirt sleeves in half. He stopped before he reached the cuffs, so that they would hold together. Now he and Patricia would be able to use the sleeves as improvised scarves.

When all of that was done, Gregory let out an exhausted breath. He felt as though he could fall down right where he was and sleep for a *week*.

"Have another brownie, Dr. Callahan," Uncle Steve said, with a weary smile. "I think you've earned it."

Gregory was starving, but he hesitated. "Don't we have to ration them and all?"

"Right now, I think you need the energy more," Uncle Steve said.

Gregory glanced at his sister for confirmation. "Patty?"

"Fine with me," she said, sounding very tired.

Gregory was too hungry to argue, although he saved one bite for Santa Paws.

The dog snapped it down, and then leaned over to lick Gregory's face in thanks. The dog's stomach was rumbling, and he hoped that they would be able to eat some more food soon. It was way past his supper time! He remembered that when he had been on his own, living outside, he had *always* been hungry. So far, this situation was terrible in the same way. He wasn't sure why any of it was happening, but he knew that he would do whatever he could to help and protect his owners. His ribs still ached, and he moved around to try to find a more comfortable position.

Uncle Steve poured some half-melted snow from one of the MRE bags into the metal cup. While he boiled it over the fire, Gregory and Patricia took turns going behind the nearest boulder to go to the bathroom. It was scary to leave their warm shelter — even to walk just a few feet away — but they felt better knowing that their uncle and Santa Paws were right nearby.

Back at the shelter, Gregory unwrapped the emergency space blanket. The package was almost as small as his hand, but the blanket was surprisingly large. It looked like a huge, paper-thin piece of aluminum foil. The blanket seemed pretty flimsy, but it would help keep them warm during the night. When it was time to go to sleep, Uncle Steve wanted the two of them to snuggle up at the back of the shelter with Santa Paws. In the meantime, he would lie by the woodpile, so he could keep the fire going throughout the night.

After the water had boiled for a few minutes, Gregory stirred in one of the cocoa packets from the MREs. It wasn't safe to drink water from the woods without boiling, or purifying, it first. Fresh snow was safer than water from streams, but they still had to be careful.

Since they only had one cup, they took turns sipping the hot drink. For the first time in hours, Gregory and Patricia could feel themselves warming up inside. When the cocoa was gone, Uncle Steve melted some more water and let Santa Paws drink it up.

The dog finished the cup and then wagged his tail.

The only sounds were the crackling of the fire, and the whistling wind. The temperature had dropped at least fifteen degrees, and it felt like it might snow.

"It's so quiet out here," Gregory whispered.

"I could play some music," Patricia offered. Her Walkman was also a tape recorder. If she disconnected her headphones, they would all be able to hear.

"Don't tell me," Uncle Steve said. "All you have is Frank Sinatra."

Gregory and Patricia smiled, although it made them sad to think about their parents. By now, they had probably arrived in Vermont — and gotten the bad news.

Gregory poked through the small pile of cassettes among their supplies. "The BoDeans," he read aloud. "Memphis Slim, Nina Simone, Harry Connick, Jr., and — the Chipmunks?"

"Nothing personal, but that is a *really* weird mix," Uncle Steve commented.

As far as Patricia was concerned, when it came to music, variety was a good thing. "There's a Joshua Redman tape, too," she said.

Gregory made a face. "Can't we just listen to the Chipmunks?"

Uncle Steve and Patricia shrugged, instead of disagreeing. The Chipmunks tape was full of Christmas carols, and they sat close together to listen to them.

Santa Paws was very intrigued by the tape recorder. He sniffed it a few times, trying to figure out where the music was coming from. Once he even poked it with his paw.

"It's okay, boy," Gregory said, and put his arm around him.

The dog wagged his tail and sat down next to him.

Listening to the Christmas carols made Gregory and Patricia feel very homesick. Right now, they were supposed to be safe in their grandparents' cabin, surrounded by the whole family.

Uncle Steve probably felt pretty lonely and afraid, too, but he didn't say anything.

"Are the planes going to come find us tomorrow?" Gregory asked.

Uncle Steve didn't answer right away. "I hope so, Greg," he said finally. "I *really* hope so."

Gregory and Patricia were too exhausted to stay awake much longer. So they crawled under the space blanket, with Santa Paws snuggling up in between them. They were both wearing their makeshift scarves wrapped across the lower half of their faces. They had also pulled their hats down over their ears so that only their eyes showed. Their jackets were zipped, their gloves were on, and they were fully dressed. Despite all of that, they were *still* cold.

"Does your arm hurt a whole lot?" Gregory asked, right before they went to sleep.

Patricia nodded. It was throbbing horribly, but she didn't want to complain. She knew that Uncle Steve was in much worse shape than she was.

"They're going to rescue us tomorrow," Gregory said confidently. "I *know* they are."

Patricia nodded again.

Then they both closed their eyes.

It was a long, bone-chilling night, and Patricia kept having nightmares. Every time she woke up, she wasn't sure where she was — or why she was so cold. Then she would see Uncle Steve keeping watch over the fire, and remember what had happened. Thinking about it only made things worse, so she just made herself go back to sleep.

She woke up for good just after dawn. When she moved, Santa Paws opened his eyes. He wagged his tail under the space blanket, and rested his muzzle on her shoulder.

She reached up to scratch his ears, and his tail wagged harder.

"Good boy," she said softly. "Don't wake Greg up."

The dog wagged his tail, and lowered his head so she would scratch his ears some more. Since his ribs still really hurt, he was glad that she hadn't patted his side.

The wind seemed stronger, and she poked her head out from underneath the blanket to see that it was snowing. *Hard.* At least four or five inches had already fallen.

She heard low coughing, and quickly turned her head toward her uncle. He was lying next to the much-smaller pile of wood, looking even worse than he had the day before. His eyes were half-closed, and his face was brightly flushed. His wallet was open, and he was staring at a picture of his wife and baby.

Patricia crawled out from underneath the

110

space blanket, being careful not to wake Gregory up. She motioned for Santa Paws to stay. He wagged his tail, nestled closer to Gregory, and went back to sleep.

"Uncle Steve?" she whispered.

He looked up dully, and tried to smile at her. "Morning," he said, and then coughed some more.

She didn't ask him how he felt, because she was afraid of what the answer would be. So she looked out at the whirling snowstorm, instead. In the meantime, Uncle Steve closed his wallet and tucked it inside his jacket.

The storm wasn't quite a blizzard, but the flakes were coming down fast. There was almost no visibility, and the winds were gusting forcefully.

"They won't be able to fly in this, will they," Patricia said.

Uncle Steve shook his head.

"Do you think it's going to stop soon?" she asked.

He shook his head.

That meant that they weren't going to be rescued anytime soon. Definitely not today, and maybe not tomorrow, either.

"If it takes them a few days, will we be able to make it that long?" she asked.

Uncle Steve glanced over to make sure that Gregory was still asleep. "We're, um — " He hesitated. "The truth is, we're in kind of a tight spot here, Patricia."

In other words, *no*. Patricia nodded.

He reached over to take her hand. "I'm sorry. I wish I could do a better job of taking care of things here."

"It's not your fault you're *hurt*," she said.

"No," he conceded. "But I'm not exactly much help, either. Look, don't worry. When the storm stops, we'll put some signals out there, and — " He let out his breath unhappily. "We'll just do our best, okay?"

It didn't even seem possible that this was the way that they were going to celebrate Christmas Eve. It seemed even less possible that they could actually *die* out here. "Do you know where we are?" she asked.

He shrugged, and then winced from the effort. "I got a little disoriented by the crash, but — yeah, more or less." He looked around, and then pointed. "If I'm right, there should be a road about five or ten miles that way."

Only five or ten miles? "That's not far," Patricia said, feeling a flash of hope for the first time since the crash. "When Rachel and I were in the Walkathon last year, we went *twenty* miles."

Uncle Steve smiled sadly at her. "Those are pretty rugged mountains out there, honey. It would be a tough haul even without all of this snow."

Maybe so, but what choice did they have? "How much longer do you think you can hold out?" she asked. "If we wait until a plane *maybe* comes, it might be — " She didn't want to say "too late," so she stopped. "I don't want to just sit here. I think we have to *do* something."

Uncle Steve nodded reluctantly, and they looked over at Gregory and Santa Paws, who were still sleeping soundly beneath the space blanket.

"I don't want to leave you here, but I don't want to send my little brother out into the forest by himself, either," Patricia said quietly.

"No, we can't do that," Uncle Steve agreed. "Even with the dog, it's too dangerous for him to go alone." He indicated her sling. "Are you in good enough shape to walk? Tell me the truth, okay?"

Patricia wasn't sure, but she nodded. "It's not so bad. I'll just be really careful."

"It's going to be even tougher than you'd imagine," he warned. "You're really going to be tired, and cold, and — "

"Do you have a better idea?" she asked.

"No," Uncle Steve said, and then he sighed. "I wish I did."

11

Once the decision had been made, there were a lot of things they had to do to get ready. Patricia woke Gregory up, and they all shared the icy can of Coke. His eyes got very big when he heard that they were going to try to hike out.

"Is it safe?" he asked.

"Our plane crashed, Greg. *None* of this is safe," Patricia pointed out.

Since that was true, Gregory nodded amiably. If she and Uncle Steve wanted him to hike, he would hike. No problem.

The first thing they had to do, was to make sure that Uncle Steve had plenty of wood to keep the fire going until help arrived. He wouldn't be strong enough to crawl around on his own, and if he ran out of wood, he would freeze.

The driving snow made it that much harder to find wood, but at least there were a lot of dead trees around. They broke off as many branches as they could reach. Other branches had fallen down during the storm, and they dragged them back to the shelter to snap into more manageable pieces.

They also tied the rope to Santa Paws' harness again, so that he could help them retrieve some of the biggest branches. To try and keep the wood dry, they stacked most of it at the far end of the shelter where it would be under cover.

While they were working, Uncle Steve had been boiling water. He heated enough to fill the two empty MRE envelopes, and then divided an envelope of the orange-flavored beverage powder between them. The resulting, diluted orange drink tasted kind of weird, but it was nice and *hot*.

Then Uncle Steve melted more water in the empty metal cup and let Santa Paws drink from it.

The dog lapped down the lukewarm water gratefully. He was *very* thirsty, and eating mouthfuls of snow only made things worse. His side hurt so much, that he was having trouble breathing, too. He drank the water so fast, that Uncle Steve refilled it two more times to make sure that he had had enough.

When Santa Paws was finished, Gregory wiped out the cup with a handful of snow. "You aren't going to make any cracks about dog germs?" he asked Patricia.

"Don't worry, I'm *thinking* them," she assured him.

While Uncle Steve gave them last-minute advice, they shared the meat loaf sandwich, some of the carrot sticks, and the last brownie. Santa Paws also had half of a Milk-Bone.

"Okay," Uncle Steve said, after drawing a crude map on his notepad. "This is approximately where we are. As nearly as I can figure, you want to head south, or southwest. There's a little compass on top of the case where the matches are."

Gregory examined the top of the little plastic tube. "The, um, needle points north?" he asked, just to be sure.

Uncle Steve nodded. "That's not going to be perfectly accurate, but it'll give you a general idea. Whenever you pass a distinctive landmark, you can write it down in the notepad. Or, if you want, you can even draw it."

Some of the advice he gave them was very complicated, and some of it was just common sense. For example, he told them that ice melted much more quickly than snow. So if they wanted to heat water, to save time, they should collect any icicles they could find. Another way to get water was to pack some snow into one of the garbage bags and put it inside their jackets.

While they walked, their body heat would start melting the snow. Then they could boil it, without wasting too much firewood.

"If you get too tired or cold, *stop*," Uncle Steve said, between bouts of coughing. "Find someplace out of the wind, light a fire if you can, and get your strength back. You want to stop *before* you get frostbitten, not the other way around."

Gregory and Patricia nodded solemnly. There was so much to remember that it was hard to keep track.

Uncle Steve wanted them to pack all of the remaining food into Patricia's knapsack, but they flat-out refused. He was going to need to keep *his* strength up, too. Finally, he agreed to keep the coffee, sugar, and cream substitute, one packet of crackers and jelly, the fruit mix, the tiny Tabasco bottle, the cough drops, and one of the packets of gum. He would also keep the empty Coke can to heat water in, while they brought the metal cup along.

They agreed that Uncle Steve would hold onto the penlight, while Gregory and Patricia kept the candle. Then Gregory wandered around the nearby trees until he found a really long sapling. He brought it back and strapped the orange life jacket to the end, so that Uncle Steve could wave it as a signal to any planes that might go by. In the meantime, he and Patricia would pack the flare.

"You kids bring the space blanket and the pocket heaters, too," Uncle Steve said. "The heaters only last a few hours, so save them until you *really* need them."

Gregory and Patricia exchanged glances, wondering if they should refuse. Wouldn't he need them more than they would?

"*End* of discussion," Uncle Steve said in a firm "hold it right there!" cop-voice.

"Yeah, but — " Patricia started.

Uncle Steve cut her off. "I have a nice, insulated shelter, and a fire going," he said. "I'll be *fine*. You two — excuse me, Santa Paws — you *three* are going to be out in the middle of it. What are you going to do, build a lean-to every time you need a break?"

The dog looked up alertly when he heard his name. They had all been talking so seriously that he thought they had forgotten him.

"How about my harmonica?" Gregory offered. "You could teach yourself to play."

"And you can read *Entertainment Weekly*. It's really good," Patricia said. "*Wuthering Heights*, too."

Uncle Steve laughed. "Okay. If you kids agree to take the Walkman, it's a deal."

Gregory packed the supplies they were bringing into Patricia's knapsack. It wasn't very heavy, and he didn't think he would have much trouble carrying it. He and Uncle Steve both put on extra pairs of Patricia's sunglasses to protect their eyes from snow blindness. Then Uncle Steve checked through the knapsack one last time, to see if they had everything they needed.

"Okay," he said, and put on a smile. "I guess that's it."

It was hard to say good-bye, and they all avoided each other's eyes. Santa Paws knew that something was happening and instinctively, he raised one paw in the point position.

"It's going to be fine," Uncle Steve said, sounding more confident than he looked.

Gregory and Patricia nodded, and kicked at the snow.

"Look, I'm going to be sitting here, and reading *Entertainment Weekly*, and having a grand old time," Uncle Steve said.

Gregory and Patricia nodded again. Patricia could feel tears in her eyes, and she quickly rubbed her glove underneath her sunglasses. Gregory just kept shifting his weight and blinking a lot.

"Come here," Uncle Steve said. He gave Gregory a quick, one-armed hug, and squeezed Patricia's good hand. "You're great kids, and I *really* love you."

"We love you, too," Patricia answered, her voice quavering a little.

"We'll go really fast, so help'll come right away," Gregory promised.

"Just be careful," Uncle Steve said. Then he reached up to pat Santa Paws. "Take care of them, boy. I'm counting on you."

The dog wagged his tail, and then barked.

"Hang onto the rope and let him break the trail for you," Uncle Steve told them. "And trust his instincts. He has better hearing, a stronger sense of smell — you name it. So, follow his lead."

With that, they all looked at each other again.

"See you soon," Uncle Steve said.

Gregory and Patricia nodded.

It was time to go.

The first few hundred yards were pretty easy. It was all downhill, and the trees protected them somewhat from the wind and snow. Santa Paws plowed along up ahead of them, the snow coming almost all the way up to his chest. His ribs felt like they were burning, but he forced himself to keep walking. Gregory and Patricia followed directly in his tracks.

With their sweatshirt-scarves wrapped across their faces, it was hard to talk. It didn't really matter, though, because they wanted to save their energy for walking. Every so often, they would pause long enough for Gregory to stick a small piece of duct tape on a tree. They wanted to mark their trail, so that any rescuers would be able to find Uncle Steve.

The ground suddenly got steeper, and they had to walk more slowly. Even though they were trying to be careful, they both kept slipping and sliding. Then Santa Paws stopped short.

"What is it?" Patricia asked.

Gregory waded forward through the snow to stand next to him, and saw that there was a ten-foot drop in front of them. There was enough snow down there so that it might be safe to jump — but it also might *not* be.

"What do you think?" he asked, when Patricia came up to join them.

She shook her head vehemently. "No way."

"It's going to take forever, if we go around," Gregory warned her.

"It's *really* going to take forever, if we both break our legs," Patricia said.

The dog waited patiently for them to decide what to do. This wasn't a very nice place to go on a walk, but if that's what they wanted, he was happy to cooperate. Even so, he would much rather be in their nice, warm house, napping underneath Mr. Callahan's desk.

His fur was covered with snow, and he shook violently to knock some of it off. The pain in his side sharpened, and he yelped once. A big chunk of snow had blown into his ear and he turned his head from side to side to try and dislodge it. His paws were also caked with snow. He lifted each one in turn and shook the icy particles away.

It was so windy on this exposed ledge that Patricia and Gregory were having trouble keeping their balance. The snow was swirling around them, and they couldn't see more than a few feet in any direction.

"Let's just keep going!" she yelled, and pointed off to the left, where the terrain appeared to slope more gently. "That way looks easier."

Gregory nodded, and turned Santa Paws in that direction.

"Come on, boy," he urged him.

The dog cocked his head, not sure where he was supposed to go.

"Find the car," Gregory told him. "Let's go find the car!" He had taught that phrase to Santa Paws to help him locate his parents' station wagon in crowded parking lots. But he could also use it here, because if Santa Paws couldn't find their *actual* car, he would always search until he found *any* car. If he knew that they were looking for the car right now, maybe he would be able to lead them to a road.

The dog sniffed the cold air and then looked at him, baffled. There definitely weren't any cars anywhere *near* here. The only scents he was picking up were things like pine trees and deer and decomposing timber. And — wait — a rabbit, maybe. Yeah, he could definitely smell a rabbit.

"Come on, Santa Paws," Gregory said. "Find the car. You can do it."

The dog wanted to make him happy, so he started making his way down the slope. The footing was very tricky, and he hesitated before each step. Gregory and Patricia were just as cautious. Sometimes, the going was so treacherous that they had to hang onto trees to keep from falling.

After a long time, they made it to the bottom of the mountain. They were in a valley now, and the ground was fairly level. But surprisingly, compared to stumbling downhill, it seemed like more work to navigate the flat terrain. Before, at least they had had gravity on their side.

It felt as though they had been walking forever. But when Gregory stopped to look at his watch after marking yet another tree with tape, they found out that it had only been an hour and a half.

"How far do you think we've gone?" Gregory asked, his breath warm against his scarf.

"Not very," Patricia answered grimly.

Gregory nodded. That was about what he had figured. He glanced up at the sky, but the snow was still coming down just as hard as ever.

Then he took out the match container and checked the little compass to see where north was. He wasn't still completely sure how it worked, but they *seemed* to be doing all right.

"We going in the right direction?" Patricia asked.

"I think so," Gregory said uncertainly. "Maybe a little bit too much east."

Patricia nodded. Either way, they were going to be heading *up*hill soon. This valley was pretty small, and mountains rose up all around them.

"Go for another half hour, and then we'll rest?" Gregory suggested. Uncle Steve had said that it was really important to pace themselves.

The thought of that was exhausting, but Patricia nodded. Somehow, they had to make it as far as they could before it got dark.

Their lives — and Uncle Steve's life — depended on it!

12

It was snowing so hard that most of the time, they couldn't really see where they were going. But Santa Paws kept plunging forward into the storm. They hung on tightly to the rope and let him lead them through the forest.

"Do you think he knows where he's going?" Gregory yelled.

"I hope so!" Patricia yelled back.

They forged on and on, through endless drifts. Sometimes the snow only came up to the tops of their boots. Other times, it was waist-deep. On top of which, they kept tripping over buried rocks and logs.

Except for the sounds of their labored breathing and the icy pellets of snow landing all around them, the woods were utterly silent. They hadn't even seen any *wildlife*.

After a while, Patricia was so cold that she was starting to stagger. Since she knew that she couldn't make it much further, she yanked on the rope to get her brother's attention.

"Greg, I have to stop for a while," she said weakly.

He was concentrating so hard on walking that the concept of doing something *else* seemed confusing.

"Just for a minute," she said. "Please?"

"Oh. Right." He looked around the dense forest, swaying slightly on his feet. "Do we just sit down where we are?"

Patricia gestured a few feet away. "Under that tree, maybe."

Gregory nodded and lurched over there.

Feeling the tug on his harness, the dog turned around. Gregory was going a different way now, so he reversed his direction and followed him. He loved his owners, but this was the *worst* walk he had ever been on. Too cold, too windy, too *everything*. And they still weren't anywhere *near* a car.

Gregory's hands were clumsy from the cold, but he unzipped the knapsack. He took out the space blanket and spread it on the ground. That way, they wouldn't have to sit directly on the snow. He started to flop down, but Patricia shook her head.

"Let's get some of this snow off first," she said.

Gregory nodded and started brushing her off.

He felt very uncoordinated and had to remind himself not to brush too hard where her arm was broken. Patricia used her free hand to knock most of the snow off him, too.

Bundled up with her face completely covered, his sister was unrecognizable. "You look like a really fat one-armed Eskimo," Gregory observed.

"*You* look like Charlie Brown's long-lost Canadian cousin," Patricia said, and paused significantly. "The *disturbed* one."

Maybe they were getting punchy, but they laughed a lot harder than either joke deserved. Then they stamped their feet over and over, trying to clear their snow-encrusted boots.

Just to be sociable, the dog shook a few times, sending a spray of snow in all directions.

Gregory and Patricia sat down on one end of the space blanket and Santa Paws squirmed in between them. Then Gregory pulled the ends of the blanket up around them. Now they were sheltered from the blowing snow, and might be able to warm up.

"I don't like nature anymore," Patricia said.

Gregory nodded. "If we make it out of this, I'm like, staying inside with Dad from now on."

They sat under the blanket, shivering. Santa Paws seemed pretty comfortable, and they both leaned close to him.

"Should we make a fire?" Gregory asked.

Patricia sighed. "That would mean we'd have to go look for wood, and figure out where to build it and all."

Right now, that sounded like *way* too much work.

"Next time we stop?" Gregory said, and Patricia nodded.

Santa Paws yawned and curled up into a tight circle. He was *really* tired. There wasn't much room, and he had to drape himself across their legs. Gregory and Patricia watched enviously as he drifted into a nap.

"He's lucky," Gregory said.

"Yeah," Patricia agreed. "We're going to have to take turns, if we sleep. Otherwise, we might freeze to death."

Gregory shuddered. After surviving all of this, that would be too awful.

Patricia changed the subject. "Let's drink our juice box. It might make us feel better."

Gregory lowered his scarf enough to grin at her. "When we sing 'My Favorite Things,' we *always* feel better."

Patricia looked right back at him. "I don't care if we *are* in the middle of nowhere. *Nothing* would convince me to sing 'My Favorite Things.' "

"I'm going to tell people you kept running down the mountains with your arms out, pretending you were Maria," Gregory said mischievously.

Patricia laughed. "Hey, if we make it out of this, you can tell people anything you want."

Gregory had been carrying the juice box inside the pocket of his hooded sweatshirt so that it wouldn't freeze. He poked the little straw inside, and they passed the box back and forth. The juice was actually fruit punch, and it was good and sweet.

"Can we listen to the Chipmunks for a minute?" Gregory asked.

Patricia nodded and fumbled for her Walkman. The batteries would probably run out pretty soon, but they might as well enjoy it until then.

They huddled under the space blanket, listening to music, and savoring every single sip of fruit punch. They weren't really warm, but at least they had stopped shivering.

Their hands and feet were so cold, that they broke down and opened one of the pocket heaters. The heaters looked like tiny white bean-bags, and there were two in each package. They were about an inch and a half wide, and three inches long. The little bags were filled with some sort of minerals, which were activated when the bag was exposed to air.

Patricia put her heater inside her one exposed glove, while Gregory immediately dropped his into his left hiking boot. After a few minutes, he switched his heater to the other boot. Patricia also transferred hers to one of her boots. When that foot had warmed up, she changed it to the other one.

She couldn't retie her boots with one hand, so Gregory had to do it for her.

"We can stop again in a while, and switch them," he said.

"Okay," Patricia agreed, wishing that they had a *hundred* little heaters and didn't have to conserve them. "Are your hands warm enough?"

Gregory nodded. "They're all right. They just feel, I don't know, kind of *thick*."

"Take them out and blow on them a little," Patricia suggested. "Or put them under your arms for a minute. That might help."

Gregory did just that until he could move his fingers pretty well again. Patting Santa Paws made them feel warmer, too. The dog opened his eyes and thumped his tail a few times.

"Ready to go back out there?" Patricia asked finally.

Gregory put his gloves back on. "Guess we don't have much choice," he said.

Patricia nodded, and they climbed out of the space blanket to face the storm again.

They walked, and walked, and walked. Slipped, stumbled, and slid. Limped, and staggered, and limped some more. Sometimes they would make it partway up on a slope, only to fall back down and have to start all over again.

Then they heard a strange rumbling sound somewhere up above them.

Gregory squinted up into the falling snow. "What's that noise?" he asked.

Patricia shrugged, too tired to pay much attention. "I don't know. Sounds like some kind of engine or something, or — " Realizing what she had just said, she stared at her brother. "Greg! It's a plane!"

He stared back at her. "What? Are you sure?"

"They're searching for us!" she said. "We're saved!" Then she began looking around frantically, trying to locate the sound. "Where are they?! Greg, come on, we have to make sure they see us!"

They were surrounded by a thick cluster of trees, and it was hard to know which way to run. This might be their only chance for survival, and they had to guess right!

"This way!" Gregory shouted.

"No, *this* way!" Patricia said, pointing uphill. "Hurry! Before they leave!"

They scrambled through the snow as fast as they could, stumbling over rocks and branches. Sensing their excitement, Santa Paws barked loudly and raced up ahead of them.

As they ran, Gregory dug the signal flare out of the knapsack, and gripped it tightly in one hand.

"Should I set it off?" he yelled. "So they'll see us?"

"Set it off *where*?" Patricia yelled back. "We have to figure out where the plane is, first!"

The vibrating sound seemed to be louder now, and Santa Paws was staring up at the sky as intently as they were.

"Come on!" Patricia said urgently. "We need to get out in the open!"

There were trees everywhere, and no sign of a clearing or lake or any other open area. The plane's engine seemed to be off to the right, and they ran in that direction. The thought of being rescued gave them so much energy that they leaped over drifts that would have exhausted them a few minutes earlier. If they fell down, they would just pick themselves up and keep running.

They still hadn't seen anything, and now, the sound of the engine seemed to be fading away. One minute, it was there; the next minute, they could only hear the wind blowing.

"Wait!" Gregory yelled. "Come back!"

They both yelled, and waved, and jumped up and down, while Santa Paws barked wildly and ran around in circles. If someone really was out searching for them, why weren't they looking more carefully? Didn't the rescue people *want* to find them?

Patricia was the first one to give up. She sank

down into the snow, trying not to cry. Not only had they not been rescued, but now that the plane had searched this area, it probably wouldn't come back.

"Down here!" Gregory kept shouting into the storm. "We're down here!" He set off the flare, and peered hopefully into the driving snow. "Come back!"

Santa Paws barked some more, and threw in a couple of howls for good measure.

"Greg," Patricia said quietly. "Take it easy. Don't waste your energy."

"But — " He glanced down at her, still waving his arms to try and get the pilot's attention. "I mean — "

Patricia shook her head. "It's too late. They didn't see us."

Gregory slowly let his arms drop, so disappointed that he almost burst into tears. Then he slumped down miserably next to her in the snow.

The plane — if there had even *been* one up there — was gone.

The afternoon crawled by. It was still snowing, although maybe not quite as hard as it had been earlier. They were both so disappointed that the search plane hadn't seen them, that they barely spoke as they slogged through the drifts. Santa Paws seemed tired, too, and his tail dragged behind him.

After a while, they stopped to crouch under the space blanket and nibble on an MRE oatmeal cookie.

"I really thought that plane was going to come save us," Gregory said miserably.

Patricia reached over to put her arm around him for a minute. "If they didn't find us, maybe they'll find Uncle Steve. At least now, we know that they're looking."

Gregory was too depressed to find much consolation in that, but he nodded.

"You want to light a fire?" Patricia asked.

"Let's just wait until we set up camp for the night," Gregory said.

Patricia was too tired to argue, so she just shrugged and ate her share of the oatmeal cookie.

Then Gregory noticed that there were ice crystals caked all around the pads on Santa Paws' feet. He took his gloves off and gently cleaned the dog's paws out. Then he rubbed his hands together and stuck them inside his jacket to try and rewarm them.

Santa Paws thumped his tail against the space blanket. His paws were cold and sore, and it was a relief to be able to rest for a while. Resting helped ease the pain in his ribs a little, too. But it still hurt to breathe, and he had to take very shallow breaths.

They sat long enough to let their body heat fill

the enclosed blanket and listen to a few Nina Simone songs. Gregory and Patricia were both yawning, and they had to fight to stay awake. Santa Paws was already dozing.

"We're going to have to set up for the night soon, Greg," Patricia said. "Put aside some time to find wood and all."

Gregory lifted his jacket cuff enough to peer at his watch. It was almost two-thirty, so they probably had about two hours of light left. "One more hour?" he proposed. "See if we can get over this stupid mountain?"

They had been climbing for a couple of hours straight now, and Patricia didn't feel as though they had made any progress.

"Okay," she said, trying to sound confident. "Let's do it."

Then they staggered back to their feet and pushed on. The ground was so steep that Gregory and Patricia were gasping for breath and their legs trembled from the effort of climbing. Santa Paws was still in the lead, but he seemed to be very tired. His ears were drooping, and every few feet, he would stop and look back at them plaintively.

"He's really losing it," Gregory said. "I'll go up front and break the trail for a while."

Patricia nodded. "Okay. We can switch off every fifteen minutes."

Gregory bent down to hug Santa Paws and

then lead him back behind Patricia. Walking in the rear would take the least energy, since he could just step in their boot prints. The dog was so exhausted that he wagged his tail forlornly and was content to follow them for now. His paws were aching, his side was throbbing, and he was weak from hunger.

The snow came up to Gregory's knees. It took so much effort to plow through the untouched drifts that he was perspiring heavily after only a few minutes.

"You all right?" Patricia asked, when she saw him start to weave a little.

Gregory nodded, too tired to respond. They were approaching a ridge running along the side of the mountain, and the wind was picking up. So much snow was pelting his face that he could barely see an arm's length away.

The snow felt crusty under his feet. Because it was so much colder on the open ridge, a sheen of ice had formed quickly on the surface of the snow. Each time he took a step, his foot crunched through and it took a lot of effort to pull it free. No wonder Santa Paws had gotten so tired!

"Can you see anything on the other side?" Patricia yelled.

Gregory couldn't really see anything at *all*. "Snow," he yelled back. "Trees."

"No gas station?" Patricia asked. "No McDonald's?"

No *anything.*

Instead of going all the way up the mountain, Gregory decided it would make more sense just to cross over the ridge and start down the other side.

There was a wide slab of snow in front of him, and he climbed up on top of it. He was just turning to tell Patricia that everything looked safe, when suddenly, the entire slab gave way under his weight.

Then, he disappeared in an avalanche of snow!

13

"Greg!" Patricia shouted, completely horrified.

Before she had time to move, Santa Paws had already bolted past her. He galloped over the side and plunged down into the gigantic pile of snow below.

When Patricia made it to the top of the ridge, she saw no sign of Gregory anywhere below. Santa Paws was about thirty feet down the slope, digging frantically through the snow with his front paws.

Realizing that her brother had been buried by what might be tons of snow, Patricia almost screamed. As she ran to help Santa Paws, she fell halfway and started sliding. She rolled right past him and had to race back up.

Being able to use only one arm to dig made her cry in frustration. She kicked at the snow with her boots, too, but Gregory was nowhere in sight.

The dog's paws were a blur of motion and snow flew behind him as he burrowed deeper and deeper. Hoping desperately that he had found the right place, Patricia dug right next to him.

If they didn't hurry, he would suffocate!

The first thing they saw was a snow-soaked jeans leg.

"There he is, Santa Paws!" Patricia shouted. "His head! We have to clear his head!"

The dog scraped the snow away from Gregory's back, trying to dig him free. He was lying face down and very still.

"I see his hat!" Patricia said. "Right there!"

Santa Paws dug so hard that he pulled the hat right off. Seeing her brother's hair, Patricia reached into the snow pit to brush the last bits from his face. Then, while Santa Paws tugged on his sweatshirt hood from behind, she used her arm and both legs to try to push him over.

Working together, they managed to move him onto his back. Gregory's face was chalky-white and his lips looked blue. Patricia was terrified that he might have been smothered, but he moved one arm feebly. Then he started coughing and spitting out snow. Some of the color was coming back into his cheeks, and Patricia breathed a sigh of relief.

"Gregory?" she asked shakily. "Can you hear me?"

"I'm really cold," he whispered, his teeth chat-

139

tering so much that he could barely form the words.

She was going to have to get him out of the wind and in front of a fire, *fast*. She scanned the slope rapidly. Snow, and trees, and more snow. A good ways down the side of the mountain, she could see what looked like a formation of rocks through the trees. It looked like their best chance.

Gregory was trying to sit up now. He moved his arms and legs experimentally, and shrugged his shoulders a few times. Santa Paws came over and licked his face joyfully, and Gregory did his best to give him a clumsy pat on the head.

"Be careful. Did you hurt anything?" Patricia asked.

"B-b-bruises and stuff," he said, stuttering from the cold.

"Okay." She was so glad to see him alive and talking that she hugged him with her good arm. "Rest here for a minute, and I'll go down to the rocks and see if I can make a shelter."

Gregory nodded, and leaned against Santa Paws to recover himself. Then, he sat bolt upright and the color drained from his face.

"What?" Patricia asked, scared all over again.

"The knapsack," he whispered, and looked around at the mammoth pile of snow around. "It's gone!"

* * *

140

Without the knapsack, they were in big trouble. Patricia started searching, but soon realized that it was a lost cause. Because the compass was attached to the top of the match container, Gregory had been carrying the matches in his jacket pocket. The only other things he had in his pockets were the Swiss Army knife and two Milk-Bones.

"I'm sorry, Patty," he said, shivering uncontrollably. "I didn't mean to — "

She hugged him again. "We'll be fine, Greg. We have the matches, so we can still build a fire. It's going to be okay." Then she held her hand out to help him to his feet.

When Gregory tried to put weight on his left ankle, his leg gave out. He gasped, and fell back into the snow.

"Is it broken?" Patricia asked, dreading his response.

"I think it's just twisted," he said weakly.

They looked at each other, both on the verge of bursting into hysterical tears.

Patricia didn't speak until she was pretty sure she could keep her voice steady. "Lift your arm around me, so I can help you down to those rocks," she said.

Gregory leaned on her heavily, unable to put much weight on his injured ankle. Then they started down the slope. Their progress was so slow that *snails* could have made it down there and back in the same amount of time.

Santa Paws moved ahead of them, thrusting his body through the snow to break a trail. Having a path to follow made it much easier to walk. Or, in Gregory's case, *limp*. Actually, Patricia was limping, too — and Santa Paws' gait wasn't all that steady, either.

Once they were inside the rock formation, the wind seemed to die down. Patricia swept the snow away from a small boulder. Then she eased Gregory onto it, so he could rest. He pulled his hood up over his head, wrapped his arms around himself, and tried to stop shivering.

Santa Paws was already climbing around the rocks and sniffing various crevices, his sides heaving from the effort of breaking their trail. He stopped in front of one and started barking.

Patricia walked over to see what he wanted to show her. She crouched down to peer into the crevice. It wasn't exactly a cave, but there seemed to be enough room for them to crawl inside. A few inches of snow had been blown through the opening, but much less than she would have expected.

"Good dog!" she praised him. "What a good boy!"

Santa Paws wagged his tail.

Gregory limped over to see what was going on.

"What do you think?" Patricia asked. "It looks safe."

Gregory nodded, shaking too hard to speak.

Patricia crawled inside first to clear aside as much of the snow as possible. It would be a tight fit in here with all three of them, but maybe they would be warmer that way.

There was a large crack at the furthest end of the crevice, and she kicked some snow over to block it. Once she was finished, she crawled back out.

"Go in out of the wind, okay?" she said to Gregory.

He was so cold that he didn't even try to argue.

Patricia decided to collect firewood first. Once Gregory was warmer, she would find some pine boughs for them to lie on. Doing everything one-handed took twice as long, but Santa Paws helped her by dragging the branches she tied to his harness. She even found a small, dead evergreen tree, and Santa Paws swiftly pulled it over to the rocks for her.

It wouldn't be safe to light the fire inside their shelter, because it would use up all of their oxygen. So Patricia doggedly kicked away the snow just outside until she reached bare rock. It wasn't very windy here, so she didn't take the time to build a firebreak.

Most of the wood was very damp, and she wasted three matches without even managing to light the tiniest twig.

"P-pine needles," Gregory said.

That was a good idea, and Patricia reached as far inside the dead evergreen tree as she could. She pulled out a thick handful of dusty needles, and scattered them around the twigs. Then, remembering the notepad Uncle Steve had given them, she reached into her inside jacket pocket.

The pages were nice and dry, and she crumpled several into tight balls of paper.

Gregory dragged himself over to the opening. "L-let me t-try," he said. "I can use both hands." His hands were shaking so much that he had trouble striking the match. But when it caught, he held the little flame to one of the wadded-up pieces of paper.

It immediately flared up, and then another one began burning. Patricia blew gently on the pine needles, hoping to make them ignite, too. At the same time, Gregory fed more wads of notepad paper into the blaze.

It took a while, but soon they had a small, steady fire.

"Can you keep it going, while I go find branches for us to sleep on?" Patricia asked.

Gregory nodded as he warmed his hands. He was still trembling, but not quite as badly as he had been before.

Patricia was in the middle of getting branches, when she realized that Santa Paws hadn't followed her.

"Santa Paws!" she called. "Come here, boy!"

When he didn't come bounding over, she assumed that he was in the cave with Gregory and went back to what she was doing. She had just dumped her second load of boughs outside the crevice, when Gregory poked his head out.

"Where's Santa Paws?" he asked, looking worried.

Patricia frowned. "I thought he was with *you*."

Gregory shook his head, and they stared at each other.

"What if he's hurt?" Gregory asked. "Maybe he fell down, or got lost, or — " Instead of finishing the sentence, he hauled himself outside. "Santa Paws! Where are you, Santa Paws!?"

They both shouted his name over and over and whistled for him. Any second, they expected him to appear, but he seemed to have vanished.

"Look, stay here," Patricia said, trying not to panic. "I'll go look for him, and — "

"If anything's happened to him — " Gregory started at the same time.

Just then, they heard the familiar sound of license tags jingling. A snow-covered shape trotted into the rock formation, his tail waving triumphantly. There was a canvas strap in his

145

mouth, and he was dragging a bulky object through the snow.

Santa Paws had found the knapsack!

They patted, and hugged, and praised Santa Paws for a long time. Delighted by all of the attention, Santa Paws wagged his tail furiously and rolled over onto his back so they would rub his stomach.

It was getting dark now, and they were happy to be warm and safe inside their rock shelter. They sat with the space blanket draped over their shoulders, thankful to be alive — and together.

Patricia had placed a garbage bag with snow inside her jacket while she was gathering wood, and by now, most of it had melted. So Gregory took out their metal cup and began boiling water. They only had one packet of cocoa left, so they only used half of it. The thin chocolate liquid tasted delicious.

When the cocoa was gone, they heated more water in the cup. Then they squeezed the bag of escalloped potatoes and ham inside and boiled it for a while. When Gregory sliced the top of the bag open, the wonderful smell of hot food billowed out.

They waited for their supper to cool a little, and then spooned out Santa Paws' share. The dog gobbled the steaming food up. Then he wagged his tail to show how glad he was to have gotten something to eat.

The ham and potatoes tasted pretty salty, but Gregory and Patricia enjoyed every bite. Having some food in their stomachs made all the difference in the world.

"You think Uncle Steve's okay?" Gregory asked.

"Sure," Patricia said, making her voice sound more confident than she felt. "We got him all of that firewood, and — he's fine. And we'll be able to get him help tomorrow, I just know it."

Gregory nodded, although he knew she was just trying to make him feel better. Santa Paws seemed to be breathing a little funny, and Gregory frowned. "Is he okay?" he asked. "Do you think he's hurt?"

Patricia watched his side rise and fall erratically. "Maybe he's just tired," she said uneasily. "He had to work really hard today."

Gregory reached forward and patted the dog gently. "Are you okay, boy?"

Santa Paws opened his eyes for a few seconds, wagged his tail, and then went back to sleep. Gregory looked at Patricia, who shrugged, and then they both settled back uneasily.

For a long time, it was quiet.

Then Patricia let out her breath. "I can't believe it's Christmas Eve," she said in a low voice.

Gregory nodded unhappily, but then suddenly

turned to look at her. "Hey! What did you get me for a present?"

She grinned at him. "I'll give you one guess."

"Sunglasses," he said without hesitating.

Patricia's grin broadened, so he knew he was right. And he *liked* sunglasses, so that was fine. He had gotten *her* a blue felt hat with a little feather in the brim.

With luck, they would get to *open* those presents sometime.

Before lying down on their pine boughs, they listened to the Chipmunks tape of Christmas carols twice, until the Walkman batteries finally wore down. After that, it was quiet again, except for the crackle of their small fire.

The wind was blowing, and somewhere off in the distance, they heard the faint howl of an eastern coyote. Santa Paws was instantly on his feet, barking. Gregory and Patricia felt scared for a minute, but they knew that Santa Paws would protect them. After a while, he settled back down underneath the space blanket, and they knew that the coyote was gone.

They tried to take turns staying awake, but sometime during the night, they both fell asleep. When they woke up in the morning, the fire had gone out. But they were still pretty warm, because Santa Paws had moved to cover them with his body when the temperature started dropping.

It had finally stopped snowing outside. Under better circumstances, the landscape would have looked like a winter wonderland. The sky was bright and clear, and all of the branches on the trees glistened with snow.

"Well," Gregory said, and sighed. "Merry Christmas."

"Yeah." Patricia tried to smile. "You, too."

By poking through the ashes of the fire with a stick, they found some glowing embers. So they got the fire going again, and made another thin cup of cocoa. They ate some crackers and apple jelly, and fed Santa Paws one of the last two Milk-Bones. Then they melted enough water for him to drink, too.

Before leaving their shelter, they put the fire out. Patricia covered the ashes with snow, just to be extra sure. Then she found a crooked stick for Gregory to lean on while he walked. His ankle was better, but he was still limping badly.

They started downhill, with Santa Paws leading the way. Refreshed from getting some sleep, they made pretty good time. Then again, walking through deep snow in the sunshine was a lot simpler than trying to make their way through a near-blizzard.

When they got to the bottom of the mountain, the ground leveled off, and they could walk without stumbling. Santa Paws stopped every so often, and sniffed the air before going on.

Sometimes he would start off in one direction, only to turn and lead them a different way. Gregory and Patricia just followed him, no matter what he did.

There seemed to be more room to walk between the trees now. Before, they had been climbing over rocks and everything. But now, the way seemed fairly clear, although the snow was still knee-deep in most places.

Patricia glanced up to her right as they were walking, and then stopped short. "Gregory, look!" she said.

Gregory followed her gaze, and saw a wooden, official-looking sign nailed to a tree. It said RESTRICTED USE AREA, and the sign had been posted by the Appalachian Mountain Club and the United States Forest Service.

"Whoa," he said nervously. "Does that mean we're trespassing?"

Patricia shook her head as a huge grin spread across her face. *Now* she understood why the path seemed easier to follow. "No. It means we're on a *trail*," she answered.

14

"So, like, we'll be in a town soon?" Gregory asked eagerly. He was so excited that he even forgot to limp for a minute.

Being on a trail meant that *some* kind of civilization had to be nearby. "I don't know," Patricia admitted. "But it has to lead to a road — or a cabin, or — I don't know. But — it's good!"

There weren't any tracks in the snow, so no one else had walked on this trail recently. Then again, December wasn't exactly the prime hiking season.

Santa Paws forced himself forward through the chest-deep snow, doing his best to make a path for Gregory and Patricia. His ribs were hurting so much now that he was panting heavily, and sometimes he coughed, too. Each step was an effort, but he just kept putting one paw in front of the other.

Gregory and Patricia were so exhausted themselves that they didn't notice how much Santa

Paws was struggling. As they all waded end-lessly through the drifts, they began to pass more small painted signs. There were arrows pointing them to different trails, and showing them how to get *back* to the mountains. Then they saw a sign that read KANCAMAGUS HWY., 1.2 MILES.

They were just over a mile away from the highway!

"Oh, boy," Gregory said, and put his arms around Santa Paws. "What a good dog!" He took the last Milk-Bone out of his pocket and gave it to him.

The dog wagged his tail and crunched his treat, still panting weakly. He wasn't sure what he had done that was so good, but the biscuit made his stomach hurt less. *Nothing* helped his ribs. He had started to catch slight whiffs of gasoline as they trudged along, but no matter how hard he tried, he *still* hadn't found the car.

When Santa Paws had finished his biscuit, he wagged his tail at Gregory and Patricia. Then he resumed his panting, unsteady trot down the snowy trail.

"Maybe we should take a turn," Patricia suggested, looking worried. "Let him rest for a while."

"Yeah," Gregory agreed. "He seems *really* tired."

First, Gregory tried to get up in front, and then Patricia tried. But each time, Santa Paws would gallop around the side until he was in the lead again.

"I guess he wants to go first," Gregory said, out of breath.

Patricia nodded, breathing too hard to answer. It certainly *seemed* that way.

They were all so exhausted that sometimes they would stumble off the trail. Then they would have to flounder around in the drifts until they stumbled back onto it. After a while, they found themselves in front of a wide area where the snow seemed somewhat grey and caved in. Santa Paws instantly stopped, and lifted one paw in the air.

"What's wrong with him?" Gregory asked.

"I don't know." Patricia limped forward to check. "Maybe he lost the trail, or — "

Before she could finish her sentence, there was a terrible cracking sound and the wet snow gave way beneath her feet! They had walked right on top of a snow-covered, partially frozen stream, and she had fallen through the ice!

The current beneath the thin crust of ice was very swift, and Patricia fought to stay afloat. Within seconds, she was so cold that her teeth were chattering and her legs and good arm were numb. Every time she tried to climb out, the surrounding ice would break away. The current was so strong that it was going to pull her underwater soon!

"Hang on, Patricia!" Gregory yelled. He started toward her, but then heard an ominous cracking underneath his boots. He froze where he was, and looked down at the ice sagging beneath his weight.

"Don't!" Patricia ordered through chattering teeth. "You'll fall through, too!"

Remembering that you were supposed to lie down and spread your weight evenly on thin ice, Gregory quickly flattened on the snow.

"Don't worry, I'm coming!" he promised.

Without hesitating, Santa Paws leaped over him and dove right into the freezing water. He swam over next to Patricia and dog-paddled in place. Patricia grabbed onto the seat belt loop on his harness, and hung on as tightly as she could. But her hand was so numb that she lost her grip and slipped underwater for a few seconds.

Santa Paws grabbed her jacket collar between his teeth and tugged her head up above the surface of the water. Patricia coughed and spluttered and gasped for air.

Gregory reached his arm out as far as he could. "Come here, boy!" he called. "You can do it!"

Santa Paws swam in his direction, dragging Patricia along behind him. She was still coughing and gasping, but she managed to grasp his harness again. Since she was hanging on now, Santa Paws released her jacket and just concentrated on swimming.

"S-s-sticks," Patricia gasped at Gregory, her voice shaking from the cold. "G-get some sticks!"

The ice sagged more as Gregory propelled himself backwards, pushing with both hands. Once the creaking sounds had stopped, he jumped up and ran toward the nearest tree. He ripped off several branches and carried them back to the ice. Then he spread them out, so that Patricia and Santa Paws would be able to grip onto something when they climbed out.

Santa Paws dog-paddled in a small circle so that Patricia would be closest to the edge of the ice. Then he pressed his body against hers, trying to push her to safety.

"Roll, Patty!" Gregory yelled. "Roll yourself up!"

Patricia tried, but she was so cold that she kept slipping back into the swirling water.

"Grab the end of a branch!" Gregory shouted. "Then I can pull you!"

With Santa Paws keeping her afloat, Patricia gathered up just enough strength for one last lunge. She was too weak to hang on, but she managed to wedge her arm around one of the branches. With Santa Paws pushing and Gregory pulling, she was able to crawl to safety. Then she lay where she was, struggling to catch her breath.

"Stay really flat!" Gregory warned her.

Patricia nodded, shivering so hard that she couldn't speak.

Santa Paws was trying to climb out of the stream, but his paws kept sliding on the ice and he would slip back into the water.

Quickly, Gregory swung one of the branches toward him. "Play tug, boy!" he yelled. "Come on!"

Santa Paws grabbed the end of the branch with his teeth in a viselike grip. Then Gregory pulled as hard as he could, until Santa Paws was able to scramble up onto the ice. He shook violently, but most of the water on his fur had already frozen into tiny icicles.

Patricia was so cold that she was having trouble standing up. Gregory helped her to her feet, and then guided her over to the nearest large tree.

"Sit down out of the wind, okay?" he said. "I'll make a fire really fast! Come here, boy! You stay, too."

Patricia nodded, hunching down into her jacket and shivering uncontrollably. Santa Paws was shivering almost as hard, and he leaned up against her. Patricia hugged him closer, trying to get warm.

Gregory piled up the driest branches he could find, and then squirted what was left of their tube of fire-starter onto the stack. There were only two matches in the match container, and the first one wouldn't light.

"What if this one doesn't work?" Gregory asked uneasily, looking at their last match.

Patricia didn't want to think about that, so she just shook her head.

Gregory took a deep breath, and then struck the match. After a tense second, it flared up and he cupped his hand around the flame so that the wind wouldn't blow it out. He brought it carefully to one of the globs of fire-starter, which sputtered, but then also started burning.

As soon as the fire was burning steadily, he began to heat a cupful of water. They didn't have any cocoa left, but he knew that it was a lot more important for Patricia to drink something *hot*, than it was for the water to taste good.

The fire was giving off a lot of heat now, but Patricia's face was very pale and she was still shivering.

"You'll feel better when you drink this," Gregory said, doing his best not to panic. "I *know* you will."

Patricia nodded feebly, and kept shivering.

Gregory was paying more attention to Patricia than he was to the tin cup, and by accident, he let his arm stray too close to the fire. His sleeve

157

burst into flames and he looked down at it in stunned horror.

"Help, what do I do?" he yelled, close to hysteria. "I'm burning!"

Patricia and Santa Paws both lunged forward weakly and knocked him down into the snow. The flames went out right away from the lack of oxygen, but Patricia and Santa Paws stayed on top of him for a minute just to be sure.

"Y-you okay?" Patricia asked through her chattering teeth.

"I think so," Gregory whispered, his heart pounding so loud in his ears that he couldn't really hear. "Th-thanks." He sat up with an effort, and examined what was left of his sleeve. The fire had burned all the way through his layers and down to his forearm, leaving a red shiny spot behind. It hurt a lot, and he pressed a thick handful of snow against it to cool the burn.

The water from the cup had spilled and put their campfire out, too. The wet branches were steaming a little, and there was smoke everywhere.

Patricia and Gregory stared at each other in a daze.

"We don't have any matches left," Gregory said, trying not to cry.

Patricia nodded, feeling a few tears of her own trickle down her cheeks.

Santa Paws whined deep in his throat, and

started pacing back and forth. Then he paused, held his paw up, and sniffed the air curiously.

"With our luck, it's p-probably a grizzly bear or something," Patricia said grimly.

Santa Paws stood very still, his head cocked to one side. Then, suddenly, he galloped away from them.

"Santa Paws, come back!" Gregory shouted after him. "You'll get lost!"

Santa Paws kept running, until he had disappeared around a curve in the trail.

Patricia grabbed a low branch on the tree and used it to pull herself to her feet. "C-come on," she said. "We'd better go find him."

Gregory nodded, and lifted her good arm around his shoulders so that he could help her walk. They followed the trail of paw prints, stumbling along as quickly as they could. Santa Paws' tracks led right out of the woods and into an unplowed parking lot. There was a small, wooden information booth, but it was closed for the season.

Just beyond the parking lot, they could see the Kancamagus Highway. Only one lane had been cleared, but it appeared to be passable.

"He did it," Gregory breathed. "He saved us!"

Patricia nodded weakly, and sank down onto a snowy picnic bench to rest.

From somewhere up on the highway, they could hear frantic barking.

"Take it easy, boy," a deep male voice was saying. "Come here, okay? I'm not going to hurt you."

Santa Paws just kept barking and racing back and forth. After all their hours of walking, he had *finally* smelled a car! Now he just had to lead the driver back to Gregory and Patricia.

Realizing that Santa Paws had found help, Gregory and Patricia staggered over to the edge of the road. They could see a snowplow idling in the middle of the highway, and a burly man with a thick blond beard hurrying after Santa Paws. He was wearing a thick blue parka and a Lincoln Sanitation Department baseball cap.

Gregory sagged against Patricia, his legs so weak that he almost fell. "We made it," he whispered, hugging her as tightly as he could.

"I know," she whispered back.

Then, they both burst into tears!

After that, everything happened fast. The snowplow driver, whose name was Andy, helped them up into the warm cab of his truck and wrapped them up in a heavy wool blanket. He had a thermos of hot coffee and Gregory and Patricia took turns drinking from the plastic cup. They were both still crying, and shivering so much that they spilled almost as much coffee as they managed to drink.

First, the local police came, followed by some

state troopers and a paramedic. Gregory and Patricia told them everything, especially where they had left Uncle Steve and how they *had* to go search for him *right away*. They both talked so fast that they kept interrupting each other, and Officer Jeffreys, the state trooper who was in charge, had to keep telling them to slow down.

Soon, they were bundled up in the back of the state trooper's four-wheel-drive Jeep. It had been arranged that their parents were going to meet them at the hospital up in Littleton. They had left as soon as they got the call, and would be there as soon as possible.

The police officers were all very nice to them, and explained that rescue planes had already been up searching all morning. Now, at least, they knew *where* to look. Gregory and Patricia just prayed that their uncle was still okay.

The ride up to Littleton seemed to take forever. Trooper Jeffreys drove, and the paramedic rode in the passenger's seat. Gregory and Patricia were too exhausted to talk anymore, and Santa Paws fell asleep across their laps.

By the time they got to the hospital, Trooper Jeffreys had to wake all of them up. There were a lot of reporters in front of the emergency room, and plenty of television camerapeople, too. As soon as the paramedic opened the back door of the Jeep, the reporters started shouting questions. Bright lights on top of the cameras were flashing, and everyone started crowding around them.

"Tell us about your ordeal!" a reporter cried out.

"Did you ever think all hope was lost?" another wanted to know.

"Where's the hero dog?" a third demanded.

There were so many people that Gregory and Patricia hung back inside the car for a minute.

"Let's clear the way!" Trooper Jeffreys said in a commanding voice. "Back off now!"

Other police officers moved forward to control the crowd, and open a path to the emergency room entrance.

Santa Paws was the first one to get out of the car. He took one tentative step forward, and suddenly collapsed. He coughed weakly, and then closed his eyes.

"Santa Paws!" Gregory gasped, and rushed forward to help him.

The paramedic scooped Santa Paws up from the ground and rushed into the emergency room with him in her arms.

"The dog went down!" she shouted. "I think he's critical!"

"Bring him into Trauma One!" one of the doctors ordered. "And I want both kids in Trauma Two!"

"We can't leave Santa Paws!" Patricia said frantically. "We have to stay with him!"

"It's all right," another doctor said, in a very soothing voice. "It's going to be fine. They're taking very good care of him."

There was a curtain between the two trauma rooms, and Gregory and Patricia could hear voices yelling about "IVs *stat*" and "Taking chest films" and that someone should call in a veterinarian, *fast*.

Gregory and Patricia refused treatment until they were sure that Santa Paws was going to be okay. The X rays showed that he had broken several ribs in the crash, and that his right lung had collapsed. He was also badly dehydrated, and suffering from hypothermia.

"Is he all right?" Gregory asked repeatedly. "Is he going to be all right?"

"He's in intensive care now," one of the nurses explained. "Don't worry, he's a good, strong dog. He'll pull through."

But Gregory and Patricia *were* worried. All those hours, Santa Paws had been hurt, and they hadn't even *realized* it. But there was nothing that they could do about that now, so they just held hands tightly, and waited for news about him.

Then, they heard two very familiar, worried voices in the front of the emergency room. Their parents had arrived!

"Where are they?" Mrs. Callahan was asking. "Please, where are our children?"

163

"Right this way," a nurse answered, and led them to Trauma Two.

As soon as they saw their parents, Gregory and Patricia started crying again. Their parents were crying, too, and hugged them over and over. Aunt Emily had come along with them, and she was smiling bravely, but her lips kept quivering.

"Santa Paws is hurt," Gregory said through his tears, as Patricia was asking if the planes had found Uncle Steve yet. "Is Santa Paws okay?"

Unfortunately, there was nothing they could do now but *wait*.

It turned out that Gregory had torn some ligaments in his ankle. The doctors made him a soft cast, and he would need crutches for about six weeks. He also had a second-degree burn on his arm, and some minor frostbite.

Patricia was also slightly frostbitten, and she was still shivering from her fall through the ice. Her knee was sprained, and she had broken her arm in *two* places. The huge cast went all the way from her fingertips to her shoulder. It hurt so much that she just kept holding on to her mother's hand the whole time she was in the trauma room. The doctors had given her a painkiller, but the only thing it had accomplished so far was to make her very sleepy.

"We really didn't want to leave him," she whispered to her mother, struggling not to cry as they waited to hear about Uncle Steve. "But I didn't know what else to do."

Mrs. Callahan kissed her gently on the forehead. "You did the only thing you *could* have done, Patricia," she said, and kissed her again. "We're *very* proud of you. Both of you."

Just then, Gregory came swinging into the room on his crutches with a big grin on his face. Mr. Callahan walked next to him, resting his hand on his son's shoulder.

"Dad and I just went to see Santa Paws," Gregory said. "He's going to be okay! He wagged his tail and everything!"

Hearing that, Patricia started crying again and hugged her mother gratefully.

As a precaution, the doctors wanted all three of them to stay in the hospital overnight. Gregory and Patricia protested, but their parents insisted. In the end, they were put together in the same room in the pediatrics ward. Santa Paws was still in intensive care downstairs, being watched by a team of local veterinarians.

The nurses brought the family a late lunch, but none of them could eat it. They were too busy worrying. Gregory and Patricia's grandparents were driving down with Miranda, and could arrive at any time.

Then, at about three-thirty, the word came in that a rescue chopper had found Uncle Steve. He was very weak, but still alive, and they were airlifting him directly to the hospital.

Aunt Emily went downstairs to the Emergency Room to wait for him. Soon, she sent word up that he was conscious, and talking, and wanted to know how *they* were.

For the first time since the plane had crashed, Gregory and Patricia relaxed. Uncle Steve was okay! They were *all* okay!

"I'm *really* tired," Patricia said to her parents.

Over in the next bed, Gregory was already asleep.

They slept until about nine o'clock that night, with their parents watching over them the whole time. When they woke up, they drank juice and ate chicken soup and chocolate pudding.

"How's Uncle Steve?" Patricia asked. "Can we go see him? And Santa Paws, too?"

"Let me find out," Mr. Callahan answered. He went out to the nurses' station, and returned with a big smile on his face. "He's awake now, and they said it would be fine."

Gregory and Patricia rode down the hallway in wheelchairs, because it was a hospital policy. But since their parents were the ones pushing them, they didn't really mind.

In addition to his collarbone, Uncle Steve had fractured his pelvis and badly strained his back. He also had some frostbite and a severe case of bronchitis. The doctors had him on lots of antibiotics, so that it wouldn't turn into pneumonia.

Gregory and Patricia's grandparents were already in the room, with Aunt Emily and Miranda. The hospital dieticians had cooked a special holiday meal for everyone, and the nurses had set up a beautiful Christmas tree in the corner of the room. It was decorated with red and green bulbs and a string of brightly twinkling lights. Someone had also found a CD player, and Christmas carols were playing in the background.

When Uncle Steve saw them come in, he put down his spoonful of Jell-O and gave them a big grin. He looked tired and frail, but he also looked extremely glad to see them.

"Well, if it isn't two of my favorite heroes!" he said.

There was a lot of noise as they all tried to talk at once, and Miranda yelled, "Yay, Daddy!" over and over. Then there was a familiar low woof, and they all turned to look at the door.

It was Santa Paws, riding on a gurney!

Gregory and Patricia both limped over to hug him, and Santa Paws wagged his tail. He was still wearing an IV in his front paw, but he looked happy and alert. He would be back to normal in no time!

"*Here's* the hero," Gregory said proudly. "All we did was follow him."

Patricia nodded. "No matter what happened, he always took care of us."

Then Gregory laughed. "Yeah. We told him to find the car, and — he found the car!"

Everyone was still laughing, and talking at once, and Santa Paws took advantage of the confusion to bark some more. Hearing all of the noise, other patients from the floor had gathered around to share in the excitement. There were also nurses and doctors everywhere, and when Santa Paws barked again, they all clapped.

"Merry Christmas!" someone yelled.

"And a Happy New Year!" someone else added.

Santa Paws kept barking and wagging his tail as hard as he could. He was overjoyed to be together with the whole family again. Somehow, in spite of their grueling adventure, they were all warm, and happy, and *safe*.

It had turned out to be a *very* Merry Christmas, after all!